St. John Harley

Eunice

A Novel. Vol. 3

St. John Harley

Eunice
A Novel. Vol. 3

ISBN/EAN: 9783337046774

Printed in Europe, USA, Canada, Australia, Japan

Cover: Foto ©Andreas Hilbeck / pixelio.de

More available books at **www.hansebooks.com**

EUNICE.

EUNICE.

A Novel.

BY

MRS. JULIUS POLLOCK,

AUTHOR OF "LISSADEL."

" Difficile est satiram non scribere."—JUVENAL.

IN THREE VOLUMES.

VOL. III.

LONDON:

TINSLEY BROTHERS, 8, CATHERINE STREET, STRAND.

1876.

LONDON:

SAVILL, EDWARDS AND CO., PRINTERS, CHANDOS STREET,

COVENT GARDEN.

EUNICE.

CHAPTER I.

Why should a man, whose blood is warm within,
Sit like his grandsire cut in alabaster.

MERCHANT OF VENICE.

"I WILL patiently and faithfully labour for her," said Harold, solemnly. "I am content to wait—I will do anything, but I cannot give her up."

"*You must—you shall!*" said Sir Peter, in suppressed tones, and trying to preserve a grave coldness. "It is not for you to decide; and I will not allow my daughter, a mere child, to engage herself to a penniless man, one whose name is stained by mercantile failure, and who is not, and never is likely to be in a condition to keep her in decent comfort."

Harold turned hot all over at these taunts, and bit his lips to keep back burning words.

" I have only to repeat what I said last evening," said Sir Peter, in bitter disdain, " our relations are at an end ; I must request you to leave Grantley at once ; I prefer your not sleeping another night under my roof."

Harold grew desperate.

" You have every right to turn me out of your house if you think proper ; but you are mistaken if you think that I will give her up. I will find means to see her."

" Ah ! you threaten !"

" When we have nothing to hope for, we

have nothing to fear," retorted the young man, sullenly.

" Zounds ! I *can't* be calm !" And again the tempest of parental indignation rained upon Harold in a hailstorm of obloquy and fury.

" I wont give her up," was all Harold said, firmly ; (he thought of his uncle's letter, but could not bring himself to mention it except as a last resource.)

" We shall see whether you will or not ; she is nothing to you, and *never shall be.*"

Sir Peter was unlike himself, there was so much decision in his watery blue eyes, and mobile mouth. In truth, he was transported out of himself by his tutor's daring and obstinacy ; and doubly angry in consequence of having discovered that Eunice shared this sentimental folly to a degree he would have deemed impossible in *his* child.

" I do not expect you to give her to me

1—?

now. Put me to any test; but *I can't* and I *wont* give her up," said Harold, setting his teeth and showing his white determined face. "Why did you let us be together if you meant to be so cruel? Did you think, because I was your boy's tutor, that I had no feelings—that I could be with her and not love her?"

Sir Peter was touched in spite of himself by Harold's evident sincerity; apart from this business he had a real liking and respect for him.

"I am disappointed—I thought I could trust you; in your selfish underhand conduct another delusion has been dispelled. You have not remembered that our first duty is not towards ourself."

"I deserve your reproaches; all the hard things you can say," said Harold, brokenly. "But it is too late now."

"You could not have made a more unfortunate choice, or more impossible. (The children **are mad,"** said the Baronet, moodily.)

Harold perceived the impression he had made, and in wild hurried words asked pardon for his intemperance, entreating Sir Peter not to let it go against his suit.

But Sir Peter **hardened** his heart ; **it** would not be doing justice **to his** child **to** entertain the idea ; **he knew how** much, **or** rather how little Harold's flimsy hopes of advancement **were** worth.

" I may seem hard, **but it** is the greatest kindness I can do **you** both. I have spoken to Eunice: **she is mad, too !** But **we shall** soon manage her when you are gone ; she will grow wiser."

The young man groaned. He felt inclined to throw every consideration of honour to the winds, and induce her to elope ; **she** might go with him **to** Ceylon. **And** then

he remembered that he had no money;
that his uncle would certainly not assist his
purpose, and that firms do not pay in advance. Although he suffered in a severe
form from Eunice on the brain, he retained
just enough common sense to recognise the
strength of these objections.

Harold got up, walked forward, and
stood close over Sir Peter.

"It is my turn now," said he, speaking
with slow determination;—"now hear me.
This letter from my uncle offers me to go
abroad for a couple of years. It is a good
business opening, and would lead in every
probability to my permanent employment
in the firm. You will see they hold out a
promise. It would put me in a position
to marry, and our wants are not extravagant. I will go, but only on one understanding—that you consent to our engagement, and that I marry her when I come

back, if I can show I have an income she and I deem sufficient."

Sir Peter read the letter attentively, and not being one of those comprehensive individuals who can do two things thoroughly at the same time, he imperfectly understood Harold's conditions. He became **quite** fatherly. This proposed expatriation **was** a godsend—worthy of his acute friend, Ralph Harnage.

" I congratulate you !—this is the very thing !"—his tone full of bonhomie. " You want complete change of scene to get this nonsense out of your head ; it may be the turning-point in your career ; your talents are wasted here," said Sir Peter, with unintentional irony.

" But I will not go unless you consent to our engagement ; on no other terms would I banish myself so long. If you refuse, I shall decline this offer, and shall

stay in England, and see her sometimes.—
Unless you mean to lock her up," said
Harold, fiercely; "and I shall consider
anything I may do fair after your treatment
of us."

Sir Peter's breast again surged to boiling
pitch, when the door opened, and Eunice
came in. Ariosto says—

> A woman for the most part reasons best
> Upon a sudden motion and untaught;
> For with that special grace the sex is blest.

Instinct was busy in Eunice that her lover
required countenance and support; a restless anxiety that broke through the natural
timidity of her social position brought her
flushed, frightened, but resolute, to her
father's side.

"This is no place for you, girl! Go to
your room!"

"But you must hear me first, father.
I will not have him sent away like this.

I am engaged to **him**; I have passed **my** word, **and** as long as I live it shall be binding as far **as** I am concerned."

Her words were brave, defiant enough, yet tears were very near the sweet dark eyes, and she trembled violently.

Harold looked as **if he could eat her.**

"**Stay where you are, sir !**" thundered Sir Peter, as Harold moved **towards her.**

Eunice flung herself on **her** knees, **and** her sobs burst forth.

"Dearest father, you **have** never refused me anything, and will you be unkind now in the one thing that will make my happiness ?"

"**You** know nothing **about** it !—what should children know ?"

" I know that I love him, **as** I shall **never** love **any one else.**"

" That I should have lived to hear a child of mine make such an unblushing assertion !

Such mean, underhand doings"—and he glared at Harold—"will come to no good! Give up this folly, Eunice : I can forgive you ; *you* are a baby—but for *him !*"—again Sir Peter's glance said things he could not trust his tongue to utter.

"He is not to blame; it is my fault," said the girl, recklessly. "I ought to have told you before ; but we only settled it last evening."

"Settled—what ?"

"That—that he told me—that we engaged ourselves," said she, incoherently. "See !—how wretched he looks ! It is unlike you to be so hard. Oh ! be kind to us—to him."

"You wish me to forget my duty, as you have forgotten yours. I cannot give you a farthing. What on earth do you expect to support existence upon ?"

"We will wait :—he is ready to go away

and work—and my thoughts will go with him, and stay with him till I die," said Eunice, passionately. "I am engaged to him, and I will *never* marry any one else !"

Sir Peter heard her with a surprise that mocks description :—he was petrified at this unexpected rebellion of his meek daughter, whom he had always considered to lack force of character. He could not wink to make sure that he was awake, his very eyelashes refusing to perform their office, and momentarily hide his glaring vision. It was a pretty thing to be a parent !—to bring children into the world for this !—that she should culminate years of anxieties by figuratively flying in the face of her natural protector ! How the deuce did all this come about ? Sir Peter asked himself in a raging perplexity. His sensible wife had been right ; why had he not

been guided by her, and eschewed learning
and fascinating instructors ?

He made an effort to assume collected-
ness; he drew a long breath, got up,
walked to the window, hummed and
hawed, and turned very red.—Then he
burst out—

"Harnage, you *must* go abroad. I ask—
I demand it of you in justice to myself and
my child. This love of which you prate so
volubly is poor stuff if it cannot stand the
test of absence. Come to me on your
return, and if you are both in the same
mind, I will lend a willing ear."

"Go abroad !" echoed Eunice, and her
face bleached, "for how long ?"

"For two years," said Harold; "but I
cannot go."

"It is a long time," said she, faintly.

"No, Sir Peter," said Harold, resolutely,
"I will *not* go, except on the distinct

understanding that she is promised to me when I return ; and that we may write to each other.—I must have something to keep me alive."

"I don't know what to do." Sir Peter never said truer words. He looked at the young man in his white heat, and thought that he had better temporize : this inconveniently ardent lover must be got rid of ; at any cost he should leave the country, a happy chance having provided the opportunity.

To dispose of him safely for two years was something : many things might chance ; "moving accidents by flood and field" might prove grisly allies—he remembered that the old adage—those who go to sea must venture—had been exemplified of late in a peculiarly lively manner. Perhaps the fevers incidental to tropical climes would remove further trouble. But the

great good to be gained by this step was
Time !—Time would bring the girl to see
the error of her views, though he began to
realize her obstinacy and her capability of
giving any amount of trouble where her
affections were concerned. Future difficulties, however, must be risked to secure
the present boon of his absolute departure
—it would never do to have him lurking
about Grantley ;—the very idea lifted his
hair until he looked an elderly porcupine.

The restiveness of the young lady in
addition to her lover's, made him incline to
pursue a timid policy. Pyke had destroyed
his nerve, and also cruelly dispelled his
belief in the infallibility of his own judgment ; consequently were the young people
indirectly indebted to that able financier
for submissions they would not otherwise
have plucked from the stern father's
breast.

Harold regarded him anxiously during this self-colloquy.

"This is a bold tone to take," and his own was modified ; "but I suppose hot-headed lovers must be excused. Go to India—madness to refuse such an offer—do well, and if you can show me when you return that you can keep her decently, she shall be yours.—I do not wish to be mercenary."

"And we may write to each other ?—you don't know what I feel at going so far away —what may happen before I come back."

"Yes, yes, you may write to her," touched by Harold's despondent tone, and his conscience smiting him with that unexpressed wish for the active agency of Yellow Fever. "You ought to be satisfied ; my concessions are enormous. I could not have believed when you came in here that I should have made them."

"I will not confine myself to useless thanks," said Harold, earnestly. "I owe you obligations which, while I live, shall not be forgotten."

"Then you are content?"

"Content is too a poor word; she is a blessing from heaven!"

"You might give me some credit for the blessing," said Sir Peter, in grim pleasantry. "There—there!—it is settled at last:—you go to-morrow. I suppose I am in your way. That child's wilfulness will make her ill," and he bustled out of the room, casting a compassionate glance at Eunice's pale, tear-stained face.

Before Sir Peter was out of the room, Harold was on his knees before her, thanking and blessing her for her goodness to him.—"His dear, brave girl!—how well she had fought their battle!"

"But what a price to pay!" she sighed.

" I don't like you to go far away ; you may never come back."

" I *must* come back. I feel invincible now, with your dear arms around me, and your kind words."

" But when you are far from both?"

" You will write to me, Eunice. I could live upon your letters ; and soon I shall come back, sweet, and then we will be married."

" It sounds strange," said she, sadly ; " it will never come to pass."

" But you love me, Eunice ? You wish to be my wife ? to live with your Harold always ?" he asked, anxiously.

" Yes ; but it is too great happiness ; we are not intended to be so happy in this world. *Don't go*, Harold. I feel that some misfortune will happen."

She became hysterical in her distress, and he had to exert all his influence to soothe

the forebodings to which she seemed a prey :
only the sight of his misgivings made her at
last smother her sorrow.

"Believe that all will be well for my
sake, Eunice ; anticipations have a trick of
fulfilling themselves."

"Yes, and I have not time to cry now,"
dashing away her tears—"I will keep them
until you are gone."

He felt almost suffocated with his grief,
his joy, and his gratitude.   Human hearts
are better schooled by happiness than
misery ;—generous and graceful virtues are
the natural offspring of the first, whilst
bitterness and unsocial passions are
born of wretchedness—he who is capable
of happiness is capable of virtue.   Harold
overflowed with gratitude to Sir Peter for
his unexpected consent to their engagement, and the sentiment restrained his
selfish promptings to urge a stolen mar-

riage, and take her to Ceylon : her love did not shrink at Poverty's dread name ;—but should he repay her father's kindness, and disinterested affection by bringing his carefully nurtured darling to discomfort and self-reproach ?—he wanted his love to prove her blessing, not her sorrow. So he subdued the fierce temptation, and tried to make light of the many thousand miles that would part them ; of the months—nay, years, that would probably elapse before they again met.

That night, when he said his prayers, he took a solemn vow that he would ever cherish Eunice ; that behave as she might to him, he would forgive her, and prove her truest friend. His heart swelled as he thought of her noble defence of him, of her faithfulness ;—he was at once the happiest and wretchedest of beings to have to leave her just when they were so madly happy together.

2—2

He could not sleep, and went out again to his old seat under her window. There was no light, and he hoped she rested, and so hoping he slept, and dreamed that she was in his arms, his own sweet wife.

CHAPTER II.

Alas ! what laws, of how severe a strain,
Against ourselves we thoughtlessly ordain.

LEO ! dear old boy !—take care of her," said Harold, almost wringing Lionel's hand off. " Don't let her be worried. I will come back—Death itself should not hold me—to see after her. Be very gentle.—My poor girl !" And he broke down, sobbing with great tearless sobs as they hurried him into the carriage.

"Contre fortune bon cœur," said Lady Grantley, kindly. " It make me grief to say the adieux—I you wish le bon voyage."

The poor fellow was almost heart-broken, though Eunice gave way most, and Harold had himself to unclasp the clinging arms

that would not let him go.—It was over !—
When and how would they meet again ?
They were in the hands of Time—the in-
sidious destroyer of all things animate and
inanimate ; the ruling power of the universe, to which all in it are subject ; which
continues its great work unceasingly, noiselessly changing the face of everything;
altering the heart, diverting the affections,
and yet all so quietly from day to day
that its inroads are permitted because they
are unnoticed.

Harold being of a confiding disposition,
took Sir Peter's compliance at more than
its worth.   That good-natured despot was
cruelly perplexed ;—he really liked the
young man, and finding it beyond him to
breast the opposition of two hot-headed
and hotter-hearted young people, he followed the motion of his heart, supported
by the best of his judgment in this consent

to Harold's wishes. Absence was the only
hope of overcoming this misplaced affection ;
it would put a period to inclinations likely,
if unchecked, to terminate in the misery of
both parties : absence was the only cure,
and therefore cheaply purchased at the cost
of any present concession ;—it was more
than probable that the future would never
call upon him to ransom his promises.

Mr. Ralph Harnage received the news
of his nephew's engagement with playful
irony ; rather as if it were a joke, and little
likely to ripen into a serious affair. Harold
was depressed by his banter, but tried to
hide it, knowing his uncle's disrelish for
aught that savoured of sentiment. On the
plea of fatigue, he escaped from his uncle's
raillery, but only to be harassed by a
strange dream that haunted him through
the night. Eunice's arms, cold and dank
as a corpse's, yet with the frantic clutch of

the drowning, clung around him. He was
trying to unclasp them all night; and he
could see nothing else—no face—no form,
only those two deathlike arms that held
him in their desperate embrace. He
smiled in relief on awakening. The night-
hag had ridden to some purpose in his
breast, taken full revenge for that hurried
late supper; the waste of waters he must
cross had cast its shadow over his visions,
and mingled with Eunice's despairing farewell. His darling was safe, and only he
would have to face the perils of wind and
waves.

Already he had tormenting fears;—she
was not over-resolute, and those surrounding her were his enemies; he regarded
them as such, feeling them to be secretly
opposed to him in this one great affair.
They would say things to his disadvantage,
and he would not be at hand to defend

himself; he left his memory an orphan, as it were, mute and friendless, to be battered by calumny and hunted by the envy of her little world. Oh! cruel fate! to take him thousands of miles away, leaving her youth and beauty unguarded by his care!

Lovers are notoriously of encroaching disposition, and already Harold repented him of the price he covenanted to pay for Sir Peter's consent. This two years' separation—could it not even now be avoided? His only hope—such a forlorn one he had been ashamed to mention it—was his miserly, crabbed old uncle, Matthew Harnage; a relative unknown to him, and who had studiously ignored his existence. Hard and miserly, his uncle might still have compassion on him; and Harold resolved to pay him a visit on his way to Southampton; he would try and interest him in his story. (Ralph Harnage was quite hopeless ; he was too fully impressed by his own merit in obtaining Harold this post abroad to listen to any vacillation.) Report said, that the miser bathed in gold. If he would only give him of his abundance—set him up in some humble fashion in London, where he might have a chance of getting on—and sometimes be able to go to Grantley !

CHAPTER III.

Gold! Gold! Gold! Gold!
Bright and yellow, hard and cold.
Spurned by the young, but hugged by the old
To the very verge of the churchyard mould.

AUTUMN, as if wishful to make amends for the indolence of her early days, had awakened to a sense of her devastating responsibilities :— the last week had made giant strides in the backward work ; bloom and beauty had been swept from the face of the earth by the desolating winds. Fled was the cheerful verdure of the fields ; and the flowery race had resigned their delicate summer robes, and hidden their diminished heads for many a month to come :—the coloured woods alone gave a richness to the land-

scape.   There is a mockery in mid-autumn,
like

A rich beauty when her bloom is lost,
Appears with more magnificence and cost,

seeking to repair with art the ravages
nature has sustained ; so do the falling
leaves, gilt and painted in splendid hues,
allure the eye only to disappoint the nearer
view.

The weather and the aspect of his uncle's
surroundings impressed Harold as omens
for the ill success of his errand.   The wind
moaned strangely as he walked up the
grass-grown road leading to Miser Harnage's abode.   It looked a God-forsaken
place ; broken steps that led to nothing ;
thickets of stunted trees, stopped in their
growth by want of care ; and the path, even
to the front door, choked by a self-planted
colony of weeds which the infrequent step
of man had been unable to subdue.   A few

sheep browsed up to the very windows of the hard square brick house ; evidently no means of turning an honest penny were neglected. The flutter of the dry leaves on the sallow grass seemed to mock his vain footsteps. However, determined to try his fortune, Harold went on, but with a failing courage that was further disturbed by the clanging bell which broke the stillness harshly.

"Is your master at home ?" he asked of an ancient damsel, whose cross eyes and puckered mouth plainly intimated that visitors were an innovation opposed to the economy of the abode.

"My master is asleep, and cannot be disturbed," said the abigail, snappishly.

"Don't you think you could manage it for me ? I wont detain him long. I am just off a journey, and have to go by the next train to Southampton, or I would not be so pressing," said Harold, his coaxing tone assisted by a judiciously administered silver pass, nor were his handsome face and sweet smile without effect.

"Well, as so be you seem civil spoken (which no one about here bees), I'll do what I can ; but I misdoubt me 'tis as much as my place is worth."

And beckoning him in, they traversed some passages which for dirt and darkness might be burrowing underground to some animal's lair, the windows, dim with the undisturbed clouds of years allowing only obscurity to penetrate the gloomy interior.

Propelled into a cavern of a room, the door shut, and deserted by the friendly handmaiden, Harold found a hiatus of boards, black with dirt and age, yawning between himself and the inhabited portion of the apartment, producing the like effect of a youth growing out of his first inexpressibles. The **small square** of carpet, that had all **been swept away except** where here **and** there a woollen tear mourned its departed nap, surrounded the fireplace, where burned slowly with cautious economy a tiny coke fire, its dull red giving only a mocking promise of heat. Over this four square inches **of** red cinder sat huddled **a** human spider—a **lean daddy-longlegs sort** of old man. Talk of having one foot in the grave!—he seemed **up to** his armpits in that debatable ground, as **if only the** greedy longing in his restless old eyes kept him from toppling in head **over** ears.

A picture—the only one that adorned the walls, was **a** satire upon—an exact replica **of the mummy figure** that **bowed over** the hearthrug—a miser in Rembrandt's gloomiest style, bending **over a** table, counting his hoard with skinny eager fingers by the glimmer of a rushlight.

He turned in his armchair on hearing the door close, and the front view of a skull-cap revealed a long sharp nose, with a square tip that gave him the appearance of a weasel—a likeness enhanced by his red-rimmed green eyes. His under lip protruded, and pressed against the upper in a way that is supposed to indicate firmness.

"To what am I indebted for this honour?" said Mr. Harnage, half rising and with a bow, a parchment smile distorting the leathery texture of his visage, which wore a resentful look at the intrusion; but his manners had a finish, and in their acme of politeness were disconcerting to his visitor.

"I am your nephew, Harold Harnage. I am going to Ceylon, and start from Southampton to-night."

"So, my fine Oxford nephew come at

last! And **may I** ask what motive has induced you to look up your old uncle ?"

" I wanted to see you before I sailed."

" Humph ! And the reason for the wish ? Pure affection, I'll be sworn ! We live in a philanthropic age." **Mr.** Harnage's face wore an expression of bitter irony, and when he smiled deep **channels became per-**ceptible around the mouth. " **But** I am forgetting that my *affectionate* nephew must need rest after the exercise of his philan-thropy," waving him to **a** chair.

Harold sat down on this invitation, his discomposure at this chilling reception aggravated by the discovery that his seat had cast its castor, and consequently re-quired careful adjustment to preserve its equilibrium.

" And you live here all alone, uncle ?"

" **Alone, young** sir—*my own choice.* **A** man who **is not a** pauper, and **has no** direct heirs, can always command the society of his affectionate relatives. But you have not yet told me the reason of *your* visit ?"

Harold winced under this plain insult, given with the cold politeness of a usurer. He rose, and, reaching his hat from the table, was about to quit his unnatural relative, in doubt whether to make the final overture of a handshake before his exit. Even Eunice would never be able to touch such an old bear ; for her dear sake he would do anything—swallow his pride ; but this was simply a hopeless enterprise.

The miser's eyes, which never quitted him for a moment, appreciated the young man's annoyance, and a sparkle of real pleasure rippled over his features.

"And your reason for coming, nephew ?" he persisted. "You did not visit me for nothing ; you must not go without telling your errand. I am a man of work, and like to see work performed."

"I came to ask your help," said Harold, bluntly. "You are my uncle, though we have never met before ; and I thought you might have some kind feeling for me. I see you have not, and am sorry I intruded, and will go."

"Well, that sounds honest at least. At whose desire, then, are you here ?—not your Uncle Ralph's ?" said Mr. Harnage, quickly, and with a vindictive glare. "*He* would not have dared to send you."

"No, he knew nothing of my intention ; nor shall I tell him."

"Rest awhile, young man," said the miser, brusquely ; "and tell me what you did come here for ? My powers are small, and I make no promises ; but words cost little, and I have leisure to listen to you."

There was something in the sharpness,

a gleam of kindliness that encouraged Harold, very different from the polite, sneering coldness.

" Well, well !" (impatiently). " Don't you hear ?—tell me about it ; that can do no harm," scanty promise in his short tones and ferrety eyes ; but Harold needed little encouragement to pour out the story of the last two months, of his love, his perplexities, and his coming exile. He could not have believed that he could speak so unreservedly of Eunice to a living creature ; but then he had never tried before, and now he found it a relief, though he had chosen a curious confidant for a love-tale. He had found it impossible to speak of her to his Uncle Ralph, with his sneering, scoffing manner ; but this dried-up old mummy appeared interested, leading him on to tell the minutest particulars by an adroit word thrown in here and there.

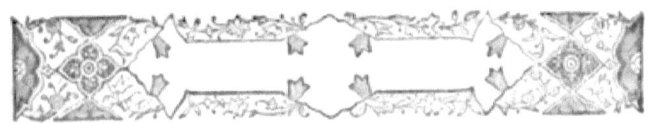

CHAPTER IV.

Come, sirs, convey me to the block of shame;
Wrong hath but wrong, and blame the due of blame.
RICHARD III.

ND she is disinterested enough to care for you—to prefer you to fine titled lovers ?—You have told her and her father that you have a rich old uncle, of course ?" And Mr. Harnage regarded Harold with a piercing suspicion that would penetrate the depths of a mental Erebus.

" I have never mentioned your existence to either of them," said Harold, proudly. " To tell the truth I did not remember it. It was a sudden thought to come to you, in the hope that you would help me to find work at home. I do not like to leave her for such a long time," a quiver of pain in his voice—his heart was very sore, thinking of his poor girl and her streaming eyes.

Apparently his uncle believed his sincerity. Abandoning that point, he asked—

" And you start for India to-night ?"

" Yes, I must go. I have no option," said Harold, despondingly, and touching his pockets, " I have empty, hungry monitors *here.* Sir Peter will not hear of my staying, unless my prospects are improved."

" And *I* have no money, if that is what you mean," said Mr. Harnage roughly, turning in fury at this appeal—the most direct Harold had ventured. " Who says I'm rich tells lies. Do I look it ?—this house—this room—this dress !" (tearing his sleeves in a sort of frenzied self-disdain). " The wealthy live in kings' palaces, I've heard, and are clothed in purple."

Harold in his desire to be politic did his best to keep the incredulity he felt on the question out of his face. The miser's humour changed; he started to his feet, tottering and shaking in his indignation. " I will not be sucked by any vampire brood ! I will keep what I have earned by hard labour, and harder self-denial. I will do as I will with my own. I will found a hospital, endow a church, and so purchase ease for my soul ; and that will be a good bargain ; and folks say, I like my money's worth." He sank back again in the well-worn leathern arm-chair exhausted by this exposition of his intentions.

Harold could not understand his quick variations, his sarcastic expressions levelled at himself as much as at his auditor.

" I am a philosopher, young man, and philosophers have no hearts—nothing so foolish. And yet there is nothing foolish

that has not been espoused by philosophers.
You have told me a story—now I will tell
you one, and we shall be quits.—I
always discharge my debts—I can't afford
to do more. I have had my romance ;—I,
too, was in love once. You sneer, young
sir !" he snarled.

Harold disclaimed the smallest intention.

" *You did*, sir, *you did!*   The notion of
this old hunks—this dried up old fossil,"
(seemingly he took delight in loading himself with ill names), "ever having any feeling
of the kind amuses you. But withered as
I am, the memory of that time *is green*,
the memory of *my wrongs is green*."

Again he started up, and walked back-
wards and forwards, gesticulating with his
long spidery hands. A hidden flame leapt
forth from the man, lighting up his lean harsh
features, and endowing the shabby ungainly
figure with a certain majesty of passion.

The fossilized **being had** become animated by hot scorching passions, hate—jealousy—fury.

" You shall hear *my* **story. There were** three young men ; or, to be more correct, there was one man whose lot **it** was never **to be young, and** two veritable young puppies, for whom life **had** ever been made easy and pleasant. **A doting mother took** care that her branches were pampered, while indulging the natural antagonism of a step-mother to the full against the eldest born. *Her* sons were handsome, lively, and spent with an open hand, winning golden opinions in return for the golden guineas they squandered. The eldest was left out in the cold ; no sweet home affection came his way, only sneers **at** his plain features and **money-loving** nature. **But** Miser Harnage, as they dubbed him even then in their heartless sport, was not slow to resent this treatment. I have always **liked to** pay my debts," he reiterated, with a satisfied **leer.**

" **I** was **left to** myself, my education **neglected,**" his voice changing to a pathos **that** spoke considerable self pity. " How often have **I** wept alone in my little room, overwhelmed by a bitter sense of loneliness and injustice. They were not healing tears ; they **froze and** hardened my nature. **But** the less they cared for me, the more I was determined to care for myself—to carve out my own fortunes."

The fire that had animated his manner sank, **his** voice became dreamy, and **he** gazed before him vacantly, seeing only what *had been.*

" **I was** fifteen years older than Philip, and was in **a** position to demand a partner- ship in the house **of** Harnage and Harnage, while he **and** Ralph **were yet mere lads.**

My father did **not** wish his partiality **to** appear, and granted my request; in substantial marks of regard he made **us** equal, but his sympathy, his affection were for **his** handsome younger boys. They grew to be jealous of this reward **of** my untiring industry, yet jeering me the while for **a** money-grubber, a machine for turning out pounds, shillings, and pence; while I made no secret of my contempt **of** the soulless unmeaning flattery that was their portion. A bitter and growing sense of the injustice **of** my treatment was a cankerworm eating into my life, and sundering every **year more and** more widely characters originally different : the same **roof covered** me **and my** brothers, but we **went our** several ways; there was nothing in common between us. **And I worked hard :** in my soul's solitude, thrown upon myself, money-getting became my religion. *Money is power*—and *I wanted* *power!*" And the miser brought his clenched fist down upon the table with a force that made the crazy legs rattle.

" I was determined to rise—not to remain the crushed worm for my butterfly brothers to flaunt their gay colours by contrast. And I succeeded. I conquered the hard callous world : what wonder if I became hard and callous in the process ! Harnage and Harnage stood higher than it had ever done ; *my* exertions helped the fond father to find funds for his Joseph's and Benjamin's extravagances for a time. At last, Ralph, the younger and ever the bolder spirit of the two, carried his irregularities a little too far—youth's frolics he gently termed them—and fearing his father's censure he applied to me, his rich steady old Timon of a brother, to help him out of the scrape. He reckoned without his host.— Not for them, nor such as they, had I toiled

and borne the heat and burthen of the day,
while **they were sunning** themselves in the
smiles of beauty and pleasure. And Ralph
vowed revenge ; idle words **I** deemed them,
but the sequel proved the blackness of his
hate. You shall hear, young man, and then
say what **claim your** father's son has upon
my pity.

"At length **my hour came. I loved !—
I** was no longer young, and **I** loved as those
can love **who have not** frittered away their
hearts on every passing **emotion.** You
start, nephew !—do you think you are going
to monopolize *all* the tender passion ? I
concede, **I** don't look much like loving now,
but I **did** then, spite the frosts of forty
winters—summers had passed **me by—I**
had none of them till *she* came. **She** was
half my age, but I loved her doubly, and
that squared the difference. **She** was gentle
and pretty, and I, poor fool ! thought her

perfect. I worshipped the ground she trod upon, I was **jealous** of the very air she breathed ; I would have poured out my life, my hopes, my gold before her ! I would have starred her dark hair with priceless gems—I, the man above such frivolities— *the miser !* Words cannot tell my infatuation for that girl; and I believed in her truth implicitly." **His** voice sank to a quaver that might be the exhaustion of age or feeling.

His nephew gave him credit for the latter state ; **yet** who would have suspected this dried-up old specimen of a covert romance, in addition to his covert and mysterious wealth—not Harold, certes. His hard face, sharp eyes, and thin-lipped mouth, with its cunning, shifty smile, were not suggestive of poetical warmth of sentiment.

A dim shadow of long-gone-by tenderness gave a charm to the meagre visage :

he **was** transformed when **thinking** of his young love. He saw the interest he had roused, and continued the recital of his wrongs.

" Let me hurry over what followed. **A** quarter of a century's striving has not brought **me** forgetfulness, though all **the** actors save two are dead. Eleanor" (Harold started violently **at the** name) " was **not** well, and went **to the Isle** of Wight : **we** were engaged, but I saw **her** seldom ; I was **a** business man, and not my **own** master. There a serpent stole into my Eden ; Ralph made her acquaintance, and intro- duced Philip to her in my absence ; Phil —the Adonis of our family, the reverse of myself, possessed of that ready grace, that winning confidence **of** manner, directly op- **posed to** my shy reserve. He fell **in love with her** ; **but it was** Ralph who fanned his treachery, and made the road easy for them, representing me in black enough colours. I was a morose, jealous miser, who would make her young life wretched. They told her that I did not love her, and she believed it! Saints above! *I*, who worshipped her every word and look! And—it was the old story—a younger Jacob, with smooth face and tongue, supplanted his elder brother. Well, I went one day to find my paradise a desert—she had eloped with your father! She dared not wait to tell me of her falsehood; she let it burst upon me like a thunderclap."

The shaking, withered man spoke with evident difficulty. An instant after, and fire again glowed in his pale eyes.

" Ralph was there, waiting to exult over me—*Sneering devil!* I struck him a blow in the face: had I carried a blade, it should have leaped into his breast!" The passionate malignity of the miser's look and words froze Harold's blood, coming from a creature so feeble, galvanized into energy only for the expression of revenge, it was appalling.

" You need not wince. I did not become a fratricide—nothing so romantic. No, I pocketed my injury and my woe ; but I swore never to see him again, never to forgive him ; and I never have—I *never will*. He thrust me beyond the pale of human sympathy ; by his means, the only woman in the whole world for me was lost to me for ever. Don't I know that your father was his weak instrument; that instigated by Ralph's subtle, sarcastic reasoning, he checked every good impulse, and closed his heart to relentings that he could not quite subdue ? Now, young sir," with an abrupt change of tone, " what would you have me do for your father's son ?—he established a sort of claim, you see, on my forbearance in aught that concerns *love-matches*" (his accents coldly measured).

" Nothing," said Harold, who was overwhelmed at these new idyls of his parents. " I should not have dared to come here had I known this."

" I could have almost forgiven the theft, had he made her happy."

" My mother died years ago ; but, boy as I was, I knew she was not happy."

"Yes," said Mr. Harnage, gleefully, " she would have done better had she taken the miser, with all his faults. Phil, the most unpractical of men, was always in difficulties ; a neglectful, contemptuous husband, he revenged his spleen on his faded wife. He stole my treasure, and then misused it, grossly misused it. And I, the rejected, had my treasure, my consolation. I made money my god—a divinity not wont to play men false. There was excitement in the pursuit, a tangible reality in the gold pieces heaped up"—his lean fingers seemed to clutch imaginary coins. " There is no artifice, no disappointment, no deceit, about gold. Gold is real —gold is power."

" My father was poor enough."

" Yes, he threw away all his advantages, and died a shameful wreck of a man, maudlin and miserable, after he had worried his wife into her grave," said Mr. Harnage, harshly. " Young man, you may go ; I am tired. I'll give you—a parting word of advice. Don't trust your Uncle Ralph ; he would sell his own son ; he never yet was faithful to a friend or generous to a foe ; wily and treacherous, he lives but to betray those who trust him."

" He may have repented his conduct to you," said Harold, apologetically ; " the rain-swollen torrent given time, may run itself pure."

4—2

"*Never!*—where the source is polluted
and springs from an evil heart : his nature
is dark. Hark ye ! another word of advice.
Take care of your young lady ; you must
be content to wait—there is naturally a
little difficulty in getting into paradise ;
and bring her to see me when you come
back from that place. A bride will be a
rare sight here. Gad ! how old Madge will
stare," and the old man's tone was quite
frisky. "Haven't you her picture to show
me ?"

Harold, mollified by the desire, produced
a photograph of his beloved.

Mr. Harnage examined it attentively.

"It is a bonnie face ; you're a lucky dog !
As you are likely to have the original, I can
keep this ; 'twill serve to remind me of my
niece elect," putting the card into his
pocket. "You can get another."

Harold was agonized.

" I cannot part with it, indeed, sir. I have no other ; she gave it to me when we said good-by, and I sail to-night."

Mr. Harnage regarded his nephew intently from under his bushy brows, and taking pity upon him, withdrew the likeness from his pocket and handed it back.

" I will get another for you," said Harold, generously.

"No, my memory is good, and will serve" (coldly). "Good-by, Master—Harold ?—is that your name ? I will not waste more of your time." And almost without a shake of the hand, Harold found himself dismissed from the inhospitable house, where he had not even been offered a glass of wine after his journey.

He told himself that he had expected nothing, and was therefore not disappointed ; yet he knew by the blank feeling

he experienced that, unacknowledged to
himself, he had cherished a warm living
hope that something would occur to do
away with the necessity for this exile.
And now Poverty with her skinny hand
drew a black veil, shutting off every ray of
hope. Matthew Harnage's heart was closed
against him; nor could Harold blame
him; it was but nature and the world's
way. Our mean actions we haste to dis-
miss from our memories; we write them in
water—not in our tears, but in shifty im-
pressionless water; while the injuries we
receive are toute autre chose, *they* are in-
scribed with an iron pen, we desire no
erasure of them from our minds. He wondered that the old man had cared to hear
of his Eunice—*his Eunice!* He craved already for a sight of her. He would go and
write to her; it was not much, but it was
something : happily he had said nothing of

this uncle ; she would not **share the agony**
of a vanishing hope.

Latterly Harold, under the enervating
influence of love, had been a mere dreamer ;
but he possessed a determined and energetic
nature, and he saw distinctly that he must
rouse himself, and act and work. It was
dreadful to leave her, but he found consolation in the belief that the best things are
most difficult to come **by.**

Matthew Harnage thought long on his
visitor, but without experiencing the slightest
inclination to prevent that same journey to
Ceylon. He was not a sleepy old gentleman, and over and over again he muttered
—" He isn't a bit like his father ; he's like
her ; he has her eyes—I seemed to see her
again in him. **Yet** there's **a** look of **Phil,**
too, about **the** mouth and brow—shifty,
weak, treacherous Phil !—this boy, though,
looks firm and honest. And he's going a

long way, and he loves. Why did he come and tell it to me? Money! money! money! They all want money: it is all they come to me for. But I think I cured him of that idea." And Mr. Harnage chuckled.

"It's all emptiness—it's all weariness," sighed the old man, drawing his chair before the battered tea-tray, on which stood a solitary cup and saucer and a little dry toast. "I heap up gold; but who shall scatter it?" Ah! who?

CHAPTER V.

The mountains look on Marathon,
And Marathon looks on the sea.—BYRON.

 WIDE gap of eighteen months
had been bridged over; long
months to many of our actors,
but notably so to our impatient lovers.
The average number of births, deaths, and
marriages had occurred, those momentous
events not however affecting our particular
friends. Outwardly things were much as
they were on Harold's departure; yet not
quite the same, for economy now held strict
rule at Grantley. The advent of this un-
welcome potentate might be traced directly
to the agency of Mr. Morell Pyke, and indirectly to the miscarriage of that gentle-

man's political career. Lord Errington had
speedily ejected his foe, unhorsed him in
the neatest manner, and quietly possessed
himself of the vacant seat—not a dissen-
tient murmur was raised in Trenton, the
loudest Pykeites having subsided into
neuters—not a few of the more energetic
spirits taking on an active voting for the
opposition.

• No one knew better than Pyke Sir
Peter's innocence and good faith (witness
his plucked condition, and the steadiness
with which he had refused tempting offers
to be enriched at the expense of others),
yet without exactly wishing to be unjust,
he made the Baronet bear the brunt of his
wounded self-love. "Arethusa Mine" had
collapsed, like many another love affair,
leaving not a wrack behind—vestiges of
broken hearts are intangible and make no
show in the account. Sir Peter had

weathered the storm **in a fashion,** but it left
him in wrecked condition, shorn of his natural defences before the liquidations, settle-
ments, and liabilities that poured in, which
would have tried the healthiest banker's
book. At the **time** when it was most
doubtful **if he could keep his head above**
water, when he **was** breasting the waves
of impecuniosity that threatened to engulf
him, **Pyke** offered **to** square matters, if
Eunice would consent to reward his devotion. Her father referred him to the
young lady, tolerably secure of her negative ;
though Pyke had become a great man—a
very great man—Sir Peter did not contemplate such an immolation of his child for a
moment.

The fertility of this master genius had
proved a well **of** ever-springing riches ;
Pyke had grown into a Colossus **of**
Finance—was deemed the incarnation of

bullion. The address of the man was marvellous; it rose and asserted itself under reverses that would have crushed a less buoyant nature. The bursting of the bubble " Arethusa Mine," his rebuff at Trenton, and such like difficulties seemed only a backbone on which he raised himself to eminence and an enviable notoriety. No longer content to play midwife to apocryphal mines and imaginary railways, he now did business on a large scale, issuing loans to States in a bad way; and the readiness with which the British public responded to his appeals doubled and quadrupled the bold originator's gains, till even he was astonished at his success.

Although Sir Peter recoiled in disgust from Pyke's eligible offer, he was greatly disquieted at the serious turn Eunice's entanglement had taken. Time was passing, and yet neither of the young people betrayed symptoms of inconstancy; apparently they had every intention of claiming that rash promise of his. **He** grew quite desperate : what could be done ? In addition to his other embarrassments was he **to be** further encumbered with a pauper son-in-law ?

We have all our various parts to play in life, and the severely determined and the inflexibly mercenary were not those originally designed **for** Sir Peter. He confessed that he made a poor show—that his future on earth was dimmed by the ever rising mist of past errors : he had allowed this great gorging greedy Pyke to fleece him mercilessly ; while his half-measures, his diplomacy, on which he prided himself, would in due time end in his girl, so sweet and good and pretty ! throwing herself away on **a tutoring** fellow—an obscure clerk in a merchant's office ! Trade

in all its bearings **was** peculiarly offensive
to Sir Peter's aristocratic prejudices.   In
these **days the** Baronet sat in ashes :
he **would not contemplate** breaking his
his word ; **if** Harold returned and claimed
Eunice, she must be his ; but he never
thought of the sacrifice without a groan ;
Jephthah was comparatively **an** enviable
parent, for Sir Peter **had no** religious
enthusiasm to support him.

Lady Grantley proved a valuable ally to
the lovers.   She had not been superior to
the "**I** told you so," which **we** all utter
with such zest to our overtaken friend, but
having used her triumph, she had thrown
her influence—none the less that she was a
silent woman—into Eunice's scale.   She
experienced none of the true maternal am-
bition that Eunice should carry her wares
to the highest **mart** ; and probably, as a
foreigner, she had always betrayed an in-

difference to, or an **ignorance of,** those finer gradations of county standing, which is **the** pied-à-terre of **a** county magnate's wife's creed.

Eunice, touched **by** the transforming finger of passion, **was** no longer **a child** caring only for the pleasure of the moment ; she had become a patient loving woman ; her voice was lower, **her** step **quieter** ; she seldom laughed, but smiled often. During this time of separation, Eunice had a great happiness, the only happiness that fills a woman's heart, the consciousness that she is loved as she loves, wholly and entirely. She was lifted above other joys and griefs ; she felt a thing apart, sanctified by Harold's love ; **a** mist divided her from all but him, and she gloried in belonging to him alone.

The restrictions caused **by the** home-poverty did not **trouble her ;** she was always **ready to** soothe and to make the

best of everything, and was more than ever
the cheerful ministering spirit of the house.
She carried about with her a panacea for
all vexations—Harold's last letters. Eunice
existed in her letters. What magic lurks
within the quiet folds of an envelope !
what life-renovating power ! Eunice had
been wont to style letter-writing the plague
of one's life, but was a convert to the belief
they had their birth in lovers' pains ; she
told him everything, and they never missed
a mail. Sir Peter chafed, but in silence ;
he would not interfere in their corre-
spondence, for his word given, he was in-
capable of falsifying it.

CHAPTER VI.

But spite of all the criticising elves,
Those who would make us feel, must feel themselves.

E shall best see how Harold fared in his tropical life, by taking a peep into his correspondence:—

" Meering, Ceylon.

" Thanks, my own dear one, for your letter; each one is sweeter, dearer than the last, for it brings me nearer to you. I am restless for two or three days before the mail comes in. I get anxious, oppressed by fears of I know not what, until I have the blessed assurance that all is well, and have your kind words to give me fresh courage. I read my letter the last thing before I sleep, and then I have happy

dreams that we are together.   I whisper
' Eunice !' and at the word, I wake ; and
the light breaks cold and bare, and my sweet
dream melts to air.

   " I cannot tell you how I weary for you
in this strange place, where there is nothing
to which the image of your beauty is linked ;
the very trees and flowers I do not care to
see, for they are not associated with you.
The vegetation in this part of the island is
grand, owing to the amount of moisture
that falls in the year.   It is the hottest
season, but we are looking for the rains to
cool us ; some such operation is becoming
necessary ; if there is a stirring of the
air, it comes so hot a blast, one imagines
its origin must be Erebus.

   " The great excitements here are elephant
hunts, but I have not been to a grand *kraal*
as yet ; the sporting does not trouble me
much.   I stay at Meering, and try to get

through my work quickly : to have a little more to do than one has time to do it in is, I find, the best thing for me now ; and I am never less alone than when alone. I am getting on famously with my new novel, for you are the angel of my inspiration—if it would only bring me fame and rupees! I begin to suspect that authorship is another name, not for genius, but for ceaseless patience.

" Will you make much of me, Eunice, when I do come back, and never tease me, and run away, as you used to do in the old days ? I shall have much to tell : you shall be the Desdemona to the thrilling recital of my adventures. I have done battle only with small deer—the scorpions and huge black spiders that we often find in the houses !—on the hottest day they make my blood run cold ! What would gentle Cowper have said of such intruders into

places sacred to repose ? The spiders are
harmless enough, but I cannot look upon
them as commendable bedfellows. I will
not afflict you by telling what I suffer from
mosquitoes, &c., but merely remark that
insect life is painfully active here, though
I have contrived to elude the leeches pretty
successfully so far."

     *   *   *   *   *

" Dearest Harold,—You ask me what
I do. I lead the laziest life. I roam the
garden till I grow weary, and then I read
and talk to father (who is much more at
home than he used to be), then drive with
Leo—we have only one horse now, we are
so poor ; but *I* do not mind it one bit, it
will teach me not to be extravagant before
we begin our housekeeping.

" After dinner, my favourite recreation is
to go to the schoolroom, and lose myself in
a reverie of what you are doing, and whether

you love me **as** well as on the day you first
told me, in the dear dingy **old room, that**
your troublesome pupil had crept into your
heart. I sit there sometimes for **I know**
not how long; and were it not for some
cruel thoughts of the hardness of fortune
that keeps you away, **I should forget there**
is **such** a thing to be done as going to bed.
But time **is passing, and the summer is**
coming ; when it comes, **this** severance will
be over ; it will all seem as **nothing then.**
Already the woods are **a carpet of yellow**
stars ; and you will be with us before they
are strewn with leaves—remember, August
is the very latest **I** give you, sir.

" I have had another admirer (for your
comfort, I speak in the past tense)—a little
melancholy man, whose modest proposals I
easily nipped. **Father was very good about**
it (that **his estate adjoined our poor acres**
is a tantalizing **fact), and also about Mr.**

Pyke, whom we do not often see; his mind
is so taken up by loans and shares that how
I ever found room there is a mystery : one
comfort is, the next new scheme will soon
crowd me out again. I cannot tell you
the repulsion that man inspires me with ;
spite his parade of friendship, I feel he is
answerable for my poor father's gloom.

"I like your lock of hair—such a boun-
teous curl! I am not minded to put it in
a locket; I will have no cold glass between
it and me. Are you well, my dearest ?
Don't work too hard, even at the book.
I wish I could sit at your elbow and hold
the pens, like Copperfield's poor little
Dora!—perhaps I shall some day !

"Tell me about the people you are with
—what the women of the country are like.
I want to know *everything*—especially what
concerns you."

* * * * *

" Hurrah ! only two **more** months, and I shall see my Eunice ! That troublesome business I came out for is in a fair way to be settled. Ward and Roberts are well satisfied **so** far, and have promised me a clerkship at 500*l.* a year, and a partnership ere long. It is a humble destiny for my pearl, but my love shall lighten it. So— the Italian has come **to grief, and** you call yourself **an** ignoramus. I **wont** have **my** wife called ugly names ; she **is** rich in womanly wisdom and in unselfish devotion. I will be her tutor in books, and she shall teach me the practical lesson—goodness, and the invaluable one—happiness ; so both shall be benefited and both taught. I know who will have **the** best of the bargain.

" **Y**ou ask about the people here : they are uninteresting, but hospitable ; I **get** more invitations than I care to accept. All nations are represented, and every variety of complexion and **costume** ; but there is a mutual distrust between the natives and the Europeans (who are principally English) ; like oil and vinegar, they wont mix. Talking to an impudent Paddy yesterday, he likened England to the upas tree, saying that her protecting arms were not less deadly than its protecting branches ; that his dear motherland had been smothered in her embrace, India withered by her touch, and Canada blighted by her approach ! Poor England ! blighting, withering, smothering—but we can bear it. *I* said nothing ; in this heat, I have only strength **to long for a** certain little English lady ; to **picture a cool** English home with plenty of **love to warm it.** When we meet, the summer will be gone, and even the ghosts of the leaves will be laid to their rest. In imagination **I picture you** as I shall next see you amid the frosts and snows, walking among the snowdrops, 'herself as modest and as pure as they.'

" I have finished my novel, and send it by this mail to Messrs. Grant and Whimper. I have called it ' Fair Victory'—may it be an omen of success !

" So—I 'tell you nothing about the ladies here !' There are none such, my pet : a few specimens of barrack hacks, half mummies with the heat (an European who attains the age of forty is regarded in the light of a patriarch) ; and as for the native fair, a Cingalese, enumerating to me his mistress's charms, said ' her eyes were like the petals of the blue manilla, her eyebrows resembling the rainbow, her hair voluminous as the tail of a peacock, her lips of the deepest richest coral, and teeth small and closely set as jessamine buds :' and to sum up her perfections, ' her nose was like the bill of a hawk.' I here cut his eloquence short, and hope that his highly-coloured portrait will answer your curiosity. I can only think of one pair of dear eyes—alas! far away. This exile is hard to bear; but time is passing, thank God! and every hour brings that bright future I see in my dreams nearer, until it be merged in a distinct visible reality.

"The scenery is enchanting, when the rain permits one to see it; but at present 'the floods are out,' and the atmosphere is a steaming vapour. When it rains, there is no mistake about it; the hill sides are a legion of running streams——

"I broke off on the discovery that a snake some three feet long was coiled up asleep on my modest bookshelf. I thought of you, and it gave me the necessary spirit for the encounter, and without allowing this philosopher in disguise further to exhibit his scientific propensities, I lent him such a thwack with a quarto volume as broke his back, and enabled me to finish at my leisure this lover of literary seclusion. My friend was a *Tic prolonga*, said to be a deadly viper. Wearied with the combat (a little exertion goes a long way in this vapour bath) — good night, my sweet. It is late, and I would rest and dream of you. Sleep consoles me. I dream that you are in my arms. Alas! I wake to find myself 3000 miles from you !"

CHAPTER VII.

The lion is not so fierce as painted.

IT came to pass in these days that Miser Harnage died and was buried. That sturdy highway-man Death had rudely called "Stand and Deliver," and the money bags had dropped from the cold, nerveless hands that could no longer clutch them.

And when in due time his will—a brief, business-like document—was read, to the measureless surprise of all concerned, it was found that he had left his accumulated riches at the sole disposal of his nephew, Harold Harnage, the son of his first and only love.

The news of this extraordinary piece of

good fortune was conveyed to the **Grant-leys in a long letter from Ralph Harnage to Sir Peter, in which he tendered his** "affectionate congratulations to his niece elect, whose disinterested affection had been above all praise :"—he said **that** "**he looked** forward to the connexion with **pride and pleasure, and only lived to see** his dear nephew in the enjoyment **of his** happiness." It was a beautiful **letter; so soothing, like** the purring of **a cat, only** there **were no** unpleasant suspicions **of claws** in the background to disturb the effect.

The amount of the inheritance was not yet known; rumour said half a million, which practical people instantly halved ; but dealing with such figures, a hundred thousand pounds more or less was a matter of little consequence. Sir Peter's delight may **be** imagined, **but not** described, and his self-gratulation was great, that he had

given his consent when Harold was poor.
His conscience pricked him touching that
same possibility of a watery death : happily
the stabs of our monitor are secret, for what
man would like to be publicly accountable
for all the thoughts that come and go—
black phantoms of the troublous night of
our fortunes ?　The whole thing was pro-
vidential : that a mysterious uncle, of whose
existence (if he had heard of it, it had not
lived in his memory) he was ignorant,
should drop from the skies, or rather it was
to be hoped ascend thither at the time of
his direst perplexity, smoothing every
difficulty by his well-seasoned and judicious
exit.　Sir Peter's fatherly affection was
already unbounded, but Eunice had changed
rôles as by magic, the suppliant of yesterday was become the goddess of to-day, with
power to dispense the blessings of prosperity.
This stroke of good luck made him a convert

to optimism ; he forgot Pyke and his vicissitudes, and in the busy laugh and sportive tongue of his children grew young again.

Lady Grantley's satisfaction was only
second to her husband's : she knew the
family embarrassments and hailed the pros-
pect of more pecunious times ; she also
cherished a kindness for Harold, and woman-
like was interested that the course of true
love should run smooth.

And Eunice—she lived in a whirl of soft
tumultuous joy. Not that she cared much
for the money ; though it was nice, every
one seemed to like it, even Leo, but it
would bring *him* home directly. Mr. Harnage had telegraphed to Harold, and received a reply, " he must remain a week or
two to finish the work he undertook, and
then for home as fast as the quickest vessel,
and wind and tide would bring him."

Then came a letter, the last and dearest ;

he was just going on board the *Albatross*. A mad letter! he was evidently wild with spirits. He should, after all, like the lord of Burleigh, be able to cover the head he loved best with priceless lace, and to shower gold and jewels into her lap. There was nothing that mind could conceive or eye desire that should not be hers. " If I live till next month," he wrote, " I shall see you! for very rapture I am almost frantic. Already I seem to feel the pressure of your head upon my breast. I shall live once more; you are the wanting half of my soul, my Eunice."

The letter was extravagantly fond, even for a lover. Not in Eunice's opinion; she thought it extremely sensible, and carried it with her always, that she might refresh herself at leisure by the perusal. Lionel declared that he feared her bodily disappearance before Harold's arrival, she floated about in such uncanny fashion as though she could scarcely keep the ground.

This honest, unselfish, faithful lover exulted in his wealth only as it could benefit her and hers. A large cheque (the first he drew) went by the same mail to his lawyer, with instructions that it should be applied to the relief of Sir Peter's most pressing necessities. He judged from Eunice's letters how grateful such help might be to the poor old man : twenty thousand pounds was a mere nothing to him now ; he neither hoped nor expected to see it again, but it was to be advanced through Mr. Sharpe (Sir Peter's lawyer) as a loan, as if from a stranger, on interest in a formal way, to save Sir Peter's delicacy.

Mr. Dodswell lost no time in carrying out Harold's instructions, seeking Sir Peter's lawyer, who readily undertook to keep his client in ignorance from whence

this golden shower emanated. The Baronet
lost himself in conjectures as to Mr. Sharpe's
unlooked for confidingness, whose bark was
worse than his bite, for the worthy man
had solemnly declared Grantley would not
carry another five thousand. He accepted
however, Mr. Sharpe's not very lucid explanation, took the goods the gods provided,
and was thankful.

The time of the *Albatross's* expected
arrival drew near, and Eunice, feverish
with expectation, could not sleep; but
happy agitation never yet hurt any one;
she looked blooming, for a gallant
ship was ever before her mind, plough-
ing the waves, and ever bringing him
nearer. Not a misgiving shadowed
anticipation; no second sight petrified her
vision with the coming woe; no echoes of
dim far-off events fell—

Deep in a darkly boding ear.

CHAPTER VIII.

The self-same heaven
That frowns on me, looks sadly upon him.
SHAKSPEARE.

CHRISTMAS was not nearly come, yet winter held its course, day by day sailing by in the cold paraphernalia of wind and frost and snow; but the gloomy weather made no incongruous accompaniment for the bright hopes that kept Eunice warm; not a foreboding chilled her.

The white-winged flakes were falling slowly; then fast and faster yet, until the air thickened, and a fairy carpet of soft feathers lay on hill and dale, every tree and shrub showing a silvery outline.

6—2

"Even the hills are dressing themselves in white for our bridal, Harold," said Eunice ; and though she spoke only to her own mirror, it reflected a vivid blush on the happy face that breathed his name. "He must come soon ; he may be nearer than we think."

But to meet or to remain separate does not depend on man : the affairs of this world have a mysterious, crooked progress, that it is impossible to calculate. Destiny, be kind ! But Destiny cannot be moved ; her dark chain is already spun, and it is winding around us all.

Eunice danced down to breakfast—a meal on which Lady Grantley seldom shed the light of her countenance. The crackling flame went merrily up the chimney, surpassing the sun in brilliancy ; the cosy, warm room more inviting than the white meadows and skeleton trees. The extreme cold held even the quick-flowing river in its staying power ; it no longer rippled on its glittering course, but lay voiceless and motionless, like a vast Titanic corpse.

" What is the matter with the river, Nicey ? is it dead ?" inquired Adrian, awe in his young voice. " Why is it so quiet and still ?"

" What do you know about death, child ?" replied his sister. " The river has only gone to sleep : soon you will see it rush along more merrily than ever."

" Look at Rip," cried Adrian. " Oh, Nicey ! see the wicked creature what he is doing !"

Eunice stepped out on the lawn to where that bold bird pursued his amusements, his blackness showing in strong relief against the expanse of snow. She found the raven disgorging pebble after pebble, which he dropped with studied precision into a hole, uttering each time a satisfied "Carack!" It was a toad that Rip was quietly stoning to death.

"There is no end to Rip's cruelty. How shall we punish him, Leo?" said Eunice, having after some trouble captured the fell destroyer and brought him indoors.

"Please yourself, and you please me," said Lionel, indifferently.

"He shall expiate his sins by learning a new word," said Eunice, determinedly; "say 'Harold.'"

Rip hung his head on one side. "Black as I am, I have too much regard for my character to say *that*," expressed in the leer of his beady eyes.

Eunice persisted in her teaching, holding choice morsels until the veteran bird became crazy with desire. He did not like it at all: over and over again he went through his whole performance, and "Choked" to an unheard-of extent. Gravel was thrown at him, he was enveloped in a tablecloth ; and she vowed he should be starved and otherwise ill-treated unless he consented to add " Harold" to the list of his accomplishments.

" How fond you are of that fellow, Eunice !" said Lionel, half enviously.

" I am fond of every one," said Eunice, joyously. (" That is a little better, Rip.") " I love the whole universe—I like even Rip, and I will kiss him." And in pursuance of this mistaken tenderness, blood was shortly seen to spurt from her coral lips.

" What do you mean to give me, 'Nice, when you come into your kingdom ? You owe me no end of gratitude ; I was a splendid gooseberry." Heretofore Lionel had observed a discreet silence on his achievements in that branch of horticulture ; but now his banter was endless on the subject of the fine lover who had proved so convenient a Crœsus. " I shall expect you to tip me a first-rate mount ; my old Sambo is not up to my weight. Say you'll do it for a fellow ?"

" I'll give you nothing—not even a new raven."

" Not when you are destroying Rip's constitution by your experiments ! Be quick with the coffee ; here's the Gov——"

" And the post," said Eunice, her father entering the room bearing a handful of those innocent-looking missives, which prove, however, often powerful engines, turning sorrow into joy, confidence into anxiety ; dimpling with smiles one face, clouding another with despair.

" No letters for me—*not one !*—it is too bad."

" Ah ! Miss Impatience, there is no news yet of Master Harold."

" Take comfort, child, in the adage, ' Ill

news travels post, but good news baits," said her father, opening a succession of deep blue envelopes, directed in clerkly hand, with a cheerfulness induced by being in funds. " It is very unlikely you will hear of the *Albatross* until you see Harnage himself. But I will look at the shipping intelligence."

" Oh, that stupid *Times !*—it never tells one anything one wants to know," said Eunice, appropriating the sheet in which centres the ladies' politics, and seeking the column where the three principal events of life jostle each other in the close proximity of Guido's pictured ugly Fates ; a startling juxtaposition to remind us that death and life go hand in hand, that from the cradle to the grave it is but a step.

Sir Peter held his modicum of the paper in tenacious grasp, spite of Eunice's longing gaze. The way of a man with his newspaper is no bad index to his character and tastes. The dabbler in speculation passes by indifferently " heavy leaders," the dull movements of foreign Powers, even the exciting record of royalty's actions, to scan with eager eyes the prices in which he is specially concerned. His avidity for intelligence quenched in the City article, Sir Peter laid down the rustling leaves that had brought him small comfort, and filled his mouth with egg and roll to try and choke the sigh he could not quite suppress.

" Lord Errington's marriage is in, I see," said Eunice, pouncing on the one oasis of interest her literature presented. " He is really married to Miss Raikes, hard and fast, by a bishop and an archdeacon, uncles of the bride. Let me have the paper, dear ; such a fashionable wedding must be honoured by a special notice."

" Your curiosity is omnivorous on the

subject of marriages," observed Leo. " But
you must not hope to compete with a
viscount in matrimonial dash."

A bright happy blush was his sister's
only answer.

" There may be some **mention** of the
Albatross. Perhaps **it has** been signalled,"
said Sir **Peter, again taking up the** paper.

Eunice sat looking **at him, her eyes**
greedy for **news, yet with a quiet,** unex-
pectant heart—the chances were **so small**
there would be mention of the ship.

Sir Peter pursued his gleanings leisurely.
It was an unusually stirring record ; the
scavengers of the world's highway had been
busy ; and he stopped to note the piquant
details **of the last scandal ;** anon was **ar-
rested by the** rumours **of** war, to finally
lose himself in the details **of the suicide of
some** hope-abandoned miserable. The confusion of subjects in a newspaper is singular

to contemplate—politics and murder, love and theft, vice and philanthropy, strange cunning, and still stranger simplicity—all huddled together in a grotesque fellowship.

Eunice had returned to her breakfast. Suddenly Sir Peter's fingers crumpled the paper convulsively. "Good God!" he exclaimed.

"What is it, father?" said Eunice, affrighted by the change in his countenance, and rushing to his side.

"The—*Albatross!*" he faltered.

"Yes, yes, speak—speak—will you?" she gasped.

"Can you bear to hear bad news?"—his lips very tremulous, and crushing the paper in his hands.

She became deathly pale.

"Not about Harold?"—her voice almost inaudible.

He nodded.

"Give it to me," said she, desperately.
"I must see it!"

"Yes, read it, my child ; you must know,
and he *may* be saved."

She made no reply ; her eyes devoured
the fatal paragraph, and a darkness fell
upon her spirit that was to know no morning.   It was one of those brief announce-
ments that are served up with our morning
meal, come upon us startling even the most
unheedful for the minute, and making the
blood recede from the cheek of the most
heartless reader—the cold, cut-and-dried
telling of a catastrophe that has hurried so
many poor creatures to eternity.

Huge letters trumpeted forth :—

"DESTRUCTION OF THE

P. & O. COMPANY'S STEAMER ALBATROSS

BY FIRE.

"The following lamentable telegram has
just been received from Madeira—

"The steamship *Albatross* destroyed by fire on the 10th of December. Two boats left her; one only has been picked up, with six men aboard; their companions died of starvation; other boat has not been heard of.

"There is, unhappily, no doubt of the authenticity of this intelligence. The rescued men will arrive at Southampton in a few days, when all particulars will be known. Great hopes are entertained that the other boat has either been picked up, or has managed to reach land."

Eunice read no further. As a mass of snow slips from its supporting bank, as silently and almost as cold, slid Eunice from her father's arms to the ground.

CHAPTER IX.

Fixed in her side she feels the painful dart,
The deadly weapon rankles in her heart.

 SHALL go mad—I shall die," said the unhappy girl, when she again opened her eyes on this troublous world, and her breath came back, laden with sighs and tearless sobs. But she did neither—sorrow does not kill so easily ; and though for days and weeks her face looked white and scared, she remained in full possession of her senses ; rather they became unnaturally acute. "The miserable have no other medicine, but only hope." She would not accept for a moment the probability that Harold was among those who had perished—Providence had been so

good to them, this agony *could not be !* She
rejected the idea with all the force of her
nature ; he was in the other boat, and it
would yet be heard of. And the way she
pored over the newspapers !—the avidity
with which she devoured the heartrending
accounts given by the rescued men !

The facts were soon told. It was in the
broad joyful light of day that a terrible
death had come and snatched into its dread
keeping more than a hundred souls. Only
six men survived the fearful hardships to
which they had been exposed, tossing about
in an open boat without provisions for many
days, to bring the tale home, and thrill the
nerves of the world by the recital of the
miseries they had endured.

It was in the hottest part of the tropics,
and the *Albatross*, all her sails set, was
skimming the calm surface of the waters,
when, towards sundown, firé broke out in

the ship, originating no one knew how. **The crew toiled and strove to extinguish the** flames, but spite their efforts the wind drove the flames straight in on deck, setting fire to the two foremost boats, and **thus** lessening the chances of escape.

The **men told** how the remaining boats **had** been rushed **at** and overcrowded, till two sank before the **eyes of those** still on the ship ; that their boat **and** another **had** alone got off, both overladen with human life till their keels **were low in the** water. **How** night had come on soon after they left **the ship,** from whose blazing, crackling **tim**bers they had had time to snatch nothing but a capacity **to** suffer. How they **had** lingered near **the burn-** ing vessel **till** daylight, **when** finding it **only** a blackened **hulk, burned** down almost to the water's edge, they moved off. The other boat **had** not been seen ; it might have drifted far away on the tide.

Eunice died a thousand deaths; her tender heart, which would have bled for the meanest man or woman there, was tortured to think of his sufferings, for she would not give up the hope that he lived, though the time that had elapsed without receiving news of the missing boat made its fate almost a certainty. She seemed to feel a conviction that Harold lived, and would yet return; and she clung to this hope for months with a tenacity that prevented her from giving way to utter despair. She steadily refused to believe in the extremity of her woe, and would put on no outward trappings of grief: but in her worn white face, which sometimes looked quite wild, and in her heavy languid steps, sorrow plainly showed.

Fled were the rosy dreams, the glowing visions on which she had surfeited; and

Hope, pale and sickly, but lingered to in-
crease her misery : it, too, were better dead,
thought her stricken father, than feeding
like a smothered fire on her heart ; better
at once suffer deepest gloom than be
mocked by its delusive ray. Each time a
letter or a newspaper arrived, so many
times did Hope gleam up from its crushed
and broken ruins, only to darken into a
fresh agony of disappointment.

They were very kind to her. Lionel was
sobered for many a day, and grew sympa-
thetic even with Adrian. Lady Grantley
put on mourning (black did not become
her)—she wished to pay " the attention to
one who was quite by far the most proper
jeune Anglais she had known." As for Sir
Peter, he really sorrowed, as his furrowed
cheeks and failing mind attested. He was
conscience-stricken, for he had sent the
young man away, coolly discounting the

7—2

chances of his never returning. And now his evil wishes, like curses, had come home to roost, they had had ruinous, wicked fulfilment :—Harold alive and wealthy would have been his comfort, pride, salvation. He felt deeply for his child, and was very tender with her. Her father's unfailing and evident strong sympathy was Eunice's great comfort; it cemented the affection between them until she felt she could do anything to please him : for his sake, she tried to overcome her sorrow, and he alone had power to win her to a smile.

CHAPTER X.

Then black despair,
The shadow of a starless night, was thrown
Over the world in which I moved alone.

 YEAR went by, and not a rumour had been heard of the missing boat from the *Albatross*. The sickening suspense, the wasted hopes that kept Eunice ever on the rack, died out—perished from pure inanition; even she ceased to think it possible that he yet lived. But the ceaseless watching month after month for one who never came told upon her, and she became so nervous that she would start at a shadow and cry out at any unwonted sound; and as the long cherished hope gradually faded, she sank

into apathy; they could interest her in nothing; she was like a flower deprived of the sun. She never mentioned him; outwardly she was calm and resigned; but she murmured and repined in secret that he had no grave, that he rested in no consecrated spot; only in her heart was his spirit enshrined for ever.

If anything could have brought her a sad comfort, it would have been the sudden, almost startling success of Harold's novel. Whether it owed its popularity to intrinsic merit, or to its being a posthumous work, or to the halo of romance surrounding its author's memory—the young clerk lost in the burning ship on his way home to claim untold wealth—"Fair Victory" was by the mighty vox populi *the* successful novel of the season—an undoubted hit.

Eunice wept till she could weep no more; if he could only have seen the realization

of his dreams!—but the tears that fall from
patient gentleness do not torture, rather
they are a healing dew. Mr. Ralph Harnage's letters, too, should have helped to
console : they were written to his old friend
Sir Peter Grantley in the most fatherly
tone of regret and abandonment to feeling
on "their common loss." "Never was
there a young man who could be less
spared swept away from his bereaved
relatives !—Resignation to the decrees
of a Higher Power could alone reconcile
him to the blow." "When time had
somewhat healed the gaping wound, he
wished to visit Grantley, to see the place
where his poor nephew had found his
keenest joy.—*Not at present ;* he could not
bear the trial ; their sharp regrets must be
first alleviated by time."

The letters were the more touching that
Mr. Harnage had **succeeded** to Harold's

legacy as heir-at-law, a state of things that was a moral on the way poor human nature's prejudices and intentions are often mocked : that Ralph Harnage should enjoy the hardly-earned savings of his ill-used brother was enough to make the miser turn in his grave. We heap up riches—*for whom?*—ah ! *whom ?*

Amid the wilderness of his crosses, Sir Peter might be thankful for one mercy— the results of some more than usually fanciful creation of financial genius had made it advisable that Mr. Pyke should put the ocean between himself and his country : though accustomed to deep waters, he had sailed a little too near the wind, and unsuspecting innocence was in a fair way to be avenged. But though the wasp departed to sunnier climes, in the Baronet's case, the insect left his sting ; the prime torturer indeed was no longer at hand to probe the wound, but he left his victim involved in debt and difficulty ; Harold's advance of twenty thousand pounds proving a mere sop in the pan, against heavy liabilities from the "Arethusa Mine" and other speculations.

Pyke's last new scheme had fallen through—not quietly, but with the éclat induced by proceedings in the Criminal Courts. The ugly words fraud and embezzlement were used freely, and some curious matters were unearthed to public view. Worse still, his riches were discovered to have no firm basis ; and Pyke, aware that there is no Lazarus so poor as Dives fallen, recognised that his sun had set irrevocably in this hemisphere. "The huge-sized monster of ingratitudes," forgetting how sweetly it had often danced to his pipings, would never again listen to the charmer's tongue. But his star might yet shine in a new world.

The event justified his aspirations. He

had taken his ingenious mind and little
else to America, and under a feigned name
was already reported to be coining dollars
out of nothing but advertisements and im-
pudence, with a sleight-of-hand and speed
that would put the expertest juggler to
shame.

Mr. Ralph Harnage did not forget the
Grantleys. True, he did not waste much
thought upon them ; he had said the right
thing, and there the matter would have
probably ended ; the charm of his new
wealth was still upon him, and summer
friends crowded thick to help to pass the
warm days of his prosperity. The little
celandines, flowers of early February, were
just opening their pale golden petals, and
sweet violets nestled on the frost-bound
banks, when it chanced that a few days'
hunting brought Ralph Harnage into the
neighbourhood of Trenton, and a curiosity

came **over** him **to see the** girl poor Harold had loved so wildly. It would be pleasant, too, to renew his friendship **with old** Peter ; and on the spur of the moment he wrote to offer himself for a few days' visit.

Sir Peter was impressed **by the** bland manners **of the** well-bred man of the world, and felt a throb of envy when he looked on the grace and symmetry which, spite of nearly half a century's wear, Ralph Harnage still preserved—flattering opinions **of** their visitor, which *he* did not at once reciprocate.

" Who would call this **girl a** beauty ?" Ralph Harnage asked himself, contemptuously. " This pale girl, **with** her listless gait, ill-arranged hair, and downcast eyes !" **Wait until you see** those **drooping lids raised, and** watch **the** tender, **sad, but** lovely eyes lighted **up** with feeling, and **the** charming mouth dimple into smiles !

For Eunice had again learned to smile.

Young and healthy people—and Eunice's physical organization was perfect—have an irresistible tendency to vanquish the ills of life. Harold's dreadful death had wrought much change in her. In Eunice's eyes all nature had been beautiful, life a measureless good; and in proportion as all had been unduly brilliant and desirable, now everything seemed to her "weary, flat, stale, and unprofitable;" for it is the sanguine temperament that suffers most severely from disappointment. She was barely twenty-two, yet the careless, irrepressible joy of youth was gone; she was indifferent to many of her old pursuits, but she was healthy—and sometimes she smiled.

Mr. Harnage skilfully spoke of Harold and his noble qualities. (It is wonderful how high our attributes grow if we have the grace to remove ourselves from this

sphere, leaving a large personalty to comfort sorrowing relatives). Eunice shrunk
at the mention ; but prepossessed in favour
of Harold's uncle, of whom he had ever
spoken in kindness, she first recognised his
right, and then melted sensibly under the
warm praise. She looked at him kindly
with her soft eyes, until Mr. Harnage re-
voked his decision as to her want of attrac-
tions, and owned that he had been hasty,
that there was a strange charm about the
girl.

Lady Grantley was confined to her room
by a slight indisposition, which threw
Ralph more on Eunice's companionship, to
his content. Forty-eight hours sufficed to
reduce this elderly Adonis to lover-like
conditions ; he took fire as easily as the
rawest recruit in Cupid's army; alike to
his surprise and joy, he found that his
pulse could still flutter at the coming of a

woman's step. His satisfaction was not unmixed; that she had been his nephew's affianced wife did not trouble *him*, but he feared that her finer susceptibilities would find it an insuperable bar to his pretensions, though the unhappy termination of her engagement, by probably doing away with the weakness ordinary to girls for romantic young lovers, made it likely that she would disregard disparity of years.

Mr. Harnage had considerable confidence in his powers; he understood women, and knew how to touch her heart : too wise to trust to accomplishing the work in his proper person, he borrowed a voice that was dear to her, and presented himself to her notice under a name that acted as a talisman—

> To show an unfelt sorrow is an office,
> Which the false man does easy.

CHAPTER XI.

Final ruin fiercely drives
Her ploughshare o'er creation.—Young.

IEU me pardonne ! Henri Bolton !"
The exclamation rose to Lady
Grantley's thin lips when she
first met Mr. Harnage, then was quickly
and resolutely suppressed, and she went
through the form of introduction, though
the startling intensity of her gaze and
nervous dilatation of her nostrils struck
even simple Sir Peter as peculiar.

Mr. Harnage on his part could not prevent a slight start, and his well-marked
brows were lifted in evident surprise.

" Have you met before ? I thought you

told me, Justine, that you had not yet made our guest's acquaintance."

"La force m'abandonne," muttered Lady Grantley, and casting an appealing glance at Mr. Harnage.

"I think—I met—your wife abroad, Grantley; many years ago," said Mr. Harnage, slowly.

"Oh! in Ardèche. Did you know her mother, Madame De Vauban?"

(Her mother!—whom had she procured to countenance the imposture?) A swift meaning look was exchanged between Ralph and the lady.

"Ah! yes—yes; a—a very charming person. I hope she continues well," with a sarcastic glance.

"My wife unhappily is now an orphan," said Sir Peter, gravely; "but we do our best to make her forget early sorrows in the land of her adoption. I will leave you to discuss bygones—I have some business matters," and with the sigh that word always invoked, he left the room.

Mr. Harnage's conduct became at once peculiar. He walked over, and carefully closed the door: then he flung himself on a sofa, and indulged in a low but hearty laugh.

Lady Grantley retreated to a window, her tall figure drawn up to its full height; her teeth clenched, and a fierce expression came into her pale eyes.

" Amorett! what in the name of all the Cupids is the meaning of this metamorphosis? What have you been doing for the last ten years ?"

" Monsieur Bolton !—quelle surprise !"

" Not so agreeable an one to you as to me, I fear," said Mr. Harnage, an unusually pleased look on his handsome features. "I am enchanted to see you,

Amorett : you are à ravir—quite like **old days.** But how **is** it I find you here— *married?* I thought Hymen's bonds were opposed to your principles." His manner was intimate, but the **veneer of** deference he generally assumed to cover **the** spirit of sarcasm with which he really regarded **women, was** remarkably thin **in** this case. His ·companion felt it to be so.

" Make not your jests at me," said she, **sullenly.** " Why you come here ? **Leave me."**

" That **is** not friendly," with one of his cold smiles. " By the merest happy chance, I discover **a** very old acquaintance in **my hitherto** invisible hostess ; and she meets me with a request to depart. Before I **obey,** I must ask Grantley to satisfy my consuming curiosity on the subject of this **love-match."**

" **You me** reproach—you man, cruel and

bad !" said Lady **Grantley**, passionately, "**mais c'est inutile** parler à **lui**" (in **lower tones**), "**he** is one stone cold-blooded."

"**I have** no wish to reproach ; seeing you brings back pleasant recollections. Let us **be** friends. I fear my French **has** somewhat rusted ; but **I** see that you have been grinding at our jaw-cracking **tongue**. Believe me, **I am** charmed **to find** you, ma chère amie, so well placed, **cherished by all the** world ; the idol **of an adoring** husband."

"Trop de bontés," said **she, uneasily.**

"And your little history ?" said **he,** banteringly, and still lolling on the sofa.

"Sare Petare a demandé **ma main**," said she, **in short, unwilling tones.**

"**And** you could **not refuse** him the **honour.** Very right. **I should** have done the same in your place" (softly clapping his hands). "**But I** always said you were **a** clever woman, though **a trifle** exigeante

8—2

and wilful. You treated me very badly, Amorett, running away without leaving me your address. However, let bygones be bygones. I bear no malice."

"Bonté divine! vous m'impatientez."

"Pardon me; allow me to crave your patience. I am about to introduce a subject of some delicacy," said Mr. Harnage, rising and coming towards her. "You have a charming step daughter, who doubtless in the sweetness of her disposition delights to render the affection and duty you could scarcely demand. Had I known the double attraction old Peter boasted, I should not have held out so long against his numerous invitations."

She did not reply, but continued to eye him steadily with a distrustful look.

"She is a charming girl," said Mr. Harnage again, and heaving a lover-like sigh; "and has taken good care of your guest during your illness. My nephew was most unfortunate to have missed his happiness. Ah ! if *I* had only twenty-five years !"

"Mais vous ne les avez pas. C'est dommage pour elle" (ironically).

"*And* for me," he rejoined in unruffled complacency. "Yet such little disparities of age are not much in these times ; they are even considered evidences of good taste. I can undertake to smooth greater diffi- culties with so able a coadjutor as your ladyship."

"Vat you mean ? I will have nothing to do in it. Nevare will you be the lover of Eunice !"

"And why, I pray you ?"

"I say not la phrase d'usage—elle est malheureuse ; elle est fidèle à Harold."

"You know as well as I do that proves nothing ; the dead cannot be mourned everlastingly."

"Mais il y a un autre obstacle invincible."

"And what is this mountain of your imagination?   Speak."

"You are the uncle of Harold."

He took this blow easily.

"A molehill, as I thought; it adds to the difficulty no doubt; but it shall be an exercise of your ingenuity to overcome it for me.   I like these contrarieties; they give piquancy to the pursuit.   You know that I never valued what I won lightly."

"Mon Dieu! qu'il est poltron!"

"You are complimentary; but let it pass.   Besides, my age and relationship will in a way benefit me.   In her romance, she would think it treachery to replace her lover with one equally young, elegant, and handsome.   My mind is made up, I cannot renounce the hope of possessing such a treasure, an angel for a companion, the purest, the most tender.   I have faith in your diplomacy that has **done so well** in les affaires de cœur."

She could scarcely endure his mocking tones : her hands clutched her neck-chain so tightly that it snapped.

"Don't break **your** chain. But I sup**pose** gold ornaments are cheap with you now ; besides, I shall be happy to present you with a substitute for **one** broken in my service. I have only confidence **in a lady's** help in an affair of this nature. **I am not** young. **I** am **no** longer good-looking, therefore **to win a** beautiful young wife I can afford **to lose** no chances, and **I** count myself fortunate in being able to command your invaluable assistance."

"*And I refuse it!*" said Lady Grantley, with sudden explosive rage. "*I will not sacrifice* the poor **child. Je n'en veux** pas. Il faut renoncer à ce mariage," lapsing into her own tongue to express the energy of her dissent.   Ralph's sneers kindled her scorn and overcame her fears.

"Ha! this is plain speaking." He came nearer, and his black eyes were sinistrous in their glare.   "Let me understand ; you really wish me to trust entirely to Sir Peter's good offices with the young lady ?"

"Why not you go your ways, and leave me alone ?" said the woman, helplessly.

"You do me too much honour.   To leave you is an exertion far beyond my virtue ; but you may count upon my friendliness and discretion."

There are men who, with hearts like icicles,can be the very mirror of politeness— can stab the soul with their cruelty, and yet at the same time assure the victim of the perfect consideration in which he is held.

"Vat you do ?"

"Do ? — *nothing* — a   mere   bagatelle,"

he answered, his cold smile worthy of
Satan. "I shall only seek from the husband the aid the wife refuses. I can offer
him some interesting domestic particulars as
the price of his influence with his daughter."

His relentless, deliberate tone carried
conviction that he would be bad as his word.

" Dieu ! si on avait un pistolet !" Her long
fingers clenched convulsively ; had a weapon
been near, Ralph's chances would have
been small.

" Happily for me, it is not the fashion in
this chill country for the fair sex to be
armed—except with charms," said he, in a
voice of easy gallantry.

" Grand Dieu ! c'est trop. Monsieur, au
nom de ciel——"

" How devout we have become !" he
sneered.

His laughing heartlessness goaded the
woman almost to madness.

"You come back in your true character, noble et désintéressé."

"Yes, I am too old to change; and we men cannot compete with you for acting. You must pardon me that I have too good a memory, and too little gratitude, madame —I should say, my lady. A defect in my constitution will not allow my sense of past favours to outweigh my longing for those to come."

"Scélérat! gredin!" she hissed, savagely.

"Fie! it is grisette to call names!" said he, mildly.

"Quelle indignité! Vat you take me for?"

"For Amorett Barras, alias Justine de Vauban (the aristocratic 'de,' I think), lately known as Lady Grantley, of Grantley Park," he replied, smoothly.

"Que deviendrai-je?" she asked, wearily.

"Think rather what you have been; the retrospect should arouse content."

"Dis-moi ?—Non, non! What would I do—interroger cet homme ?" quickly interrupting herself.

"We have strayed some way from the business in hand," said Mr. Harnage, tired of the pastime which had afforded him considerable amusement. "Adieu! I shall go seek mine host: it is always a pleasure to be the first to enlighten a friend on the subject of his mistakes," walking to the door with an air of callous resolve.

"Que faire!—que dire! Ah! save me from the shame to blush at the eyes of my husband. It will him kill."

"Not at all; we men are made of sterner stuff. The esclandre would not be beneficial for *your son*, certainly."

The shot took effect; she turned paler and trembled.

"O ciel! j'oublie le pauvre enfant!"

"Forget him no longer. Consider the poor child, and his blighted name. You love your child?"

"Love him?—love my Adrien? C'est comme la manne du désert à mon cœur aride! Vat you wish me to do?" And for the first time she became supplicating.

"Ah! now we are getting to be more sensible. You, a woman, and not know how to compass your end, and that end —matrimony! I love Eunice!"

"*You love!*"

"It is my caprice, then—what you will —to marry her. Eunice is to be my wife within six months. I am rich, and can therefore make myself acceptable to the father. It will be a good thing for her; a girl whose engagement has ended unfortunately, and who has no *dot*, will not do badly in becoming my wife."

"You understand make **the** bargain," said **Lady** Grantley, . **scornfully.** "You **do well to** make cheap **what you** would **buy."**

"**No** senseless delays, remember!" **said** he, sternly. "**In six** months—I give **you** not **a** day **longer—you** can easily manage that decrepit **partner of yours."**

"**Pas un** mot **contre lui!** I **not it** hear. C'est mon bienfaiteur."

"An involuntary **one;** he had **no** idea of the **extent of the** rehabilitation. **My** amiable friend, au revoir! I relieve you of my presence." And waving his hand grace-**fully, Mr.** Harnage terminated the inter-**view.**

CHAPTER XII.

He must needs go that the Devil drives.

EFT alone, Lady Grantley stood rooted to the spot, gazing at the door as if she expected his re-appearance.

"Demon! Scoundrel! Gredin! Coquin!" She heaped on him every word she could think of, a pot-pourri of select French and English terms of opprobrium. "Enfin il est parti.—Je suis seule! Am I mad?" striking her forehead. "Is it a bad dream to see again that man affreux? to meet him *here*—ici! J'éprouvais, depuis un quart d'heure, des mouvements de dépit et de fureur. Vat to do? Unhappy woman!

—all goes bad ; il n'y a que moi—moi seule que la **fortune semble poursuivre**—même dans ce séjour calme **et** contente. **My head** is a fire—je brûle—I **not** able **to think.** **That** man has no pity ; do I not know it well ? **I** must do as he say for the sake **of** my poor boy. And Eunice—I have **pity** for her with this man terrible. Mon cœur pleure pour toi, petite."

She knew Ralph **Harnage, and felt a** shuddering pity for **the poor girl** who must be handed over to his **tender** mercies.

" No, I will not. I care not for myself— he shall do his worst. Yet he can ruin me— **my** child—Sare Petare !—all are **in his** power. And he is rich to help our distress. **We** have lost much with **ces** rentes—ces **chances fatales.** Et Sare Petare is good ; **he not** me accuse that I **him** urged **à ces** speculations. **Mais,"** clasping her hands as though addressing **a** judge, " c'était d'abord dans l'intention la plus pure, la plus louable, pour former une fortune pour mon Adrien. It is always like that ;—nous autres femmes, ce sont les bonnes intentions qui nous perdent. Dieu ! l'on vient——"

Lady Grantley pursued her self-communion in the sanctity of her room, though she almost feared to look steadily at the hues of her own ideas. When they flitted before her fancy like fearful masks arising uncalled for, she strove to tear herself from the contemplation of their aspect, to interpose between her inward eye and them masses of ordinary conceptions. She had lied and schemed to escape a bad life to which she had been condemned when little more than a child, and successful in her schemes and her lies, she had tried faithfully to do her duty in her new sphere. The womanly feeling that remained to her had been cherished into stronger life by her quiet, honoured life at Grantley, and she shrunk from an exposure that would be worse than death to her husband with his sensitive pride.

She reflected until the exigences of her position blinded her to the cruelty of pressing this marriage, and expediency re-assumed its regal sway. It was essential that Eunice should marry a man of fortune, and why not this one? Harold gone, she stood nearly as fair a chance of content with Ralph as with another. Besides, however willing *she* might be, probably her power would not be strong enough to bring this union about ; at least there could be no harm in lending it her support, and in the face of that, successful or otherwise, even such a wretch as Ralph Harnage, seeing her sincerity, would scarcely wish to betray her.

Lady Grantley joined her family almost reconciled to the part cruel fate forced her to play, for already the presence of her evil genius was deadening the good that was in her. It is wonderful how untoward circumstances will warp the intellect—how capable the human mind is of subversion; like woody fibre submitted to the action of a petrifying stream, it gradually assimilates the qualities of its associates.

Ralph Harnage's sentiment for Eunice was the strongest and most pleasing he had experienced for years, and it increased as he saw more of her. Fallen spirits sometimes glance back with regret to the heaven they have forfeited. Perhaps Mr. Harnage looked upon Eunice, in her innocent sweetness, as one who could renew for him the paradise of early days. Though quick in deciding, he was firm of purpose, and prompt to execute, and his cool judgment and habit of steadily pursuing his plans generally overcame

obstacles, and attained his ends. He
argued that, the first natural embarrass-
ment over, Eunice would admit him to a
friendship she would not dream of according to a younger man. Nor did he draw
this deduction without reason; though if
Eunice had suspected the source of his
attentions, she would have revolted; but
the poor child thought that his consideration, his devotion to her every word and
look, was from pity at her bereavement,
the outpouring of his fatherly affection for
Harold, and this drew her sympathies
towards him : she even took herself to
task for the relief she felt at his departure,
and declared her opinion to every one with
an unnecessary amount of emphasis, that
" Mr. Harnage was a *remarkably agreeable*
man."

Mr. Harnage was too wise to pursue
his success beyond the limits of prudence,

and did not attempt to act the lover on this visit; but secure in Lady Grantley's co-operation, left his ally to prepare the ground before his speedy reappearance. The confidence was not misplaced; having once recognised the necessity of the sacrifice, she was not one to waver. She approached the subject carefully and at leisure.

"Vous êtes bien changé, ma chère enfant; you lose your good features with this always fret. I cannot see her so troubled, so pale, sans pitié," added her ladyship, as if to herself.

The sunlit eyes were indeed overclouded, and the rosy lips seldom laughed and no longer spoke the glad fancies of youth. The ready tears coursing down her cheeks were Eunice's only answer.

"It is useless to fret for what is gone past the hope," remonstrated her stepmother, kindly. "You yourself should resign to the will of Heaven."

"Oh! cant of comfort," said Eunice, inwardly. "I must be wretched all my life."

"And you still love that other one, petite?"

Eunice felt mingled surprise and anger at these inquiries. As if she ever could forgot her tender, patient, loving Harold!

"Why do you ask?"

"Because you are admired, which you should be; and if you fret always your beaux jours will go."

"And leave me on your hands! It is a heavy burthen that you must bear. I am sorry for you, but it cannot be helped." She spoke bitterly.

"Mais, ma petite, I would see you happy."

They mocked her. Harold gone, it

was no longer hers to give or to take happiness.

"For your dear father—for your family, you should make the effort. Here is a man rich, powerful, good, who loves you to distraction. I give here de sages conseils, what I would take for myself. Monsieur Ralph Harnage——"

Eunice fled from the room with a sort of breathless, passionate murmur, cutting the thread of her stepmother's eloquence short. However, the ice had been broken, the tiny seed planted; careful watering and attention would yet nourish it into a tree bearing good or evil fruit, as the case might be.

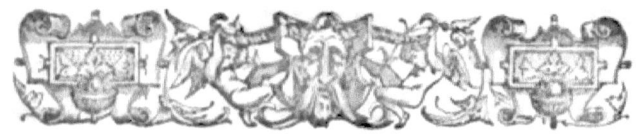

CHAPTER XIII.

Come forth—and pass **away**! This is the great command of Nature—nothing remains—nothing is un-changeable, but change.—BEUZENBERG.

N this free country no one is sup-posed to be wed against her will, and we are apt at speaking in scornful disapprobation of the arranged marriages in vogue with our continental neighbours. There are several other ways, · however, of forcing people into matrimony. Persuasion, if cunningly used, is mightier than coercion. Ridicule, too, is a powerful agent with the young: give way to its en-croachments, and reason becomes paralysed, right and wrong mere words which convey nothing but confusion to the mind that

throws courage and firmness to the winds when it stoops to the low dominion of *ridicule.*

None but a woman can measure the efficacy of unceasing taunts on fidelity to a shadow—to a lover long dead; the reproaches on the selfishness that would not assist a father and a brother. By bringing forward the good and suppressing the evil, there is no line of action that may not be made to appear desirable. Lady Grantley employed every means in her power. She painted in the darkest colours the dismal futurity before the family if Eunice refused her aid, and worked on the girl's feelings by dilating on Sir Peter's failing health, caused by anxiety. And she tried, but with small success, to gain over her husband and Lionel to join their entreaties with hers to forward this match: they understood Eunice's repugnance to a marriage with a near relation of her lost lover, and would **not influence** her for or against **it**.

Ralph Harnage had come **and gone many times** (Lady Grantley took **care** that he should have opportunities to plead his cause) ; but **his wooing did not speed ;** Eunice was firm in her refusal, and too indifferent and heartsick to heed her **step-mother's** arguments.

" Love's Labour's Lost" not being a play to Mr. Harnage's taste, he meditated retiring altogether from **the** field. **He was on** the point **of** raising **the** siege, his **only** doubt whether in doing so he should, in Parthian fashion, discharge **a** poisoned arrow, scattering desolation on Grantley by revelations concerning its mistress, when another and more **powerful** lever than his influence over **Lady Grantley** came into his hands.

It will not be forgotten that Harold's first act on finding himself to be a man of property had been to advance on favourable terms twenty thousand pounds to Sir Peter Grantley. Mr. Dodswell had waited patiently until any reasonable hope that his client survived was over, and now wrote to inform Ralph Harnage that the debt had lapsed to him, and inquiring Mr. Harnage's pleasure ; whether it was his wish that Mr. Sharpe should be pressed for the money, or if he desired to continue the loan on the same terms.—The small interest exacted, according to Mr. Harold Harnage's instructions, had been punctually paid, the Baronet being still in ignorance as to the lender.

Mr. Harnage clutched the letter, and triumph shone in his black eyes. By means of that bit of paper he could crush them all ; he seemed to feel Eunice in his grasp, but there was little lover-like soft-

ness in his expression. He knew that
Grantley was heavily burthened ; there was
not a chance of Sir Peter's being able to
raise the sum. The next hour saw **him**
in Mr. Dodswell's private room—the next
train landed him at Trenton.

Unnecessary to follow the use Mr. Harnage delayed not **to** make of his new
instrument ; he worked it skilfully and
with a will. " No one could be **more un-**
willing to press an old friend. If he might
be allowed to help in extricating Sir Peter
from any little embarrassments, it was the
dearest privilege to assist relations." Then
he adverted warmly to his affection for
Miss Grantley. Sir Peter could not com-
plain of the manner or the matter, **and yet**
he felt as if he were caught in a trap. The
necessity for payment was not done away
with because the debtor used forbearing
words—words that bore a cruel double

meaning. He could not blind himself to the state of the case. He owed a large sum of money to this man ; he could not pay ; and he was asked—*politely*—but he was asked for an equivalent, which it was in his power to hand over.

No help for it now ; Eunice must marry Ralph Harnage ; but it was hard—life always was hard for him. When his re-grets for Harold were keenest—when the knowledge of the young man's generous, delicate assistance touched him deeply, his hard fortune constrained him to this slight of his memory, compelled him to put a pressure on his child's inclination.

True, it was desirable that Eunice should marry ; true, also, that a very jeremiad of lamentation would not bring the lost man back to life ; true, again, that Sir Peter thought no ill of Ralph. Had he done so, he would have cut out his tongue rather than advocate **the** marriage. **Still,** though **he even had** a leaning **towards** Ralph as his **old** friend, and also strongly wished to see Eunice provided **for, this** world-stained man, and double the age of his sweet innocent child, **was not one** whom he would have chosen. **But** Eunice was twenty-two, she **had** no fortune, cared to go nowhere; **and the** gentle sombre depression which was her usual state was little likely to attract suitors. Then there was that largest consideration—that twenty thousand pounds which he **could not pay**! Fate **had** settled everything for him as usual, and as usual settled **it** contrarily.

He told her **all, and left** it for **her** decision.

Eunice **was more** remarkable **for** simplicity and tenderness than for her passion and sublimity: clannish **attachment and** a soft yieldingness were the leading traits

of her character. **She** had thought sadly
that the accidents of life could no longer
touch her ; but

> One fire burns out another's burning,
> One pain is lessened in another's anguish.

"If I were to coin my life's blood, I
could not find this money," her father had
said to her, his haggard sunken eyes filled
with tears. "My dear, Mr. Harnage is
inclined to be very generous to me, to you,
to all of us. It is a weary world, but we
must make the best of it. You will want
a protector when I am gone. And poor
Leo is not like other men, he cannot work
for his living."

And then he had cried and maundered—
"he was a wretched man ; he wished it
could have been different." And Eunice
knew that he thought of Harold, and her
heart was softened for her father's troubles, and her tears fell, too, and mingled

with his, as she laid her face on his shoulder, and faltered that, "he could count upon her doing in this and in all things according to his desire."

Loving and sensitive, and easily influenced through her affections, Eunice trusted in those she loved with a perfect faith. Unconscious of her own worth, she was ready to yield up her life if it would benefit her father, who had been so good to her and to Harold. And so tinselled over, decked as it were in a sacrificial garb of family affection, Eunice brought herself to contemplate an union from which she had recoiled with what she deemed an unconquerable repugnance, and came to think that possible which had seemed impossible, and allowed herself to be drifted into a vortex of misery that must swallow her up.

Women are riddles, swayed alternately

by passion, reason, **caprice**, instinct ; perhaps the latter is their safest guide. Well
for Eunice had she followed her instinct,
and said " No" to Mr. Harnage's suit ; but
passion and caprice were dead within her
—were no longer motive powers ; and
reason, apparently the surest counsellor,
clamoured that she ought to accept him.
Our natural resource when distressed and
lonely is in philosophy—we begin to specu-
late on man and his destiny. Eunice's
philosophy, on which she had declined,
taught her that the poor remnant of her
life was of nothing worth ; it therefore
could signify little what became of it, how
it was passed, or into what custody she
gave it. The beauty of her life had departed, she was thrust out from the garden
of Eden, and would be a wanderer until
she died ; as well give the dregs of her
jaded life to this one as to another ; she no
longer hoped for happiness in a world

where misery **held its court**, where virtue was to be sold and distress bought.

She reasoned **thus,** striving the while **to** subdue the repulsion **to Mr. Harnage** which had sprung up at the first whisper **of** marriage. But in vain **she** schooled herself with **the** remembrance that he **had** cared **for** Harold's **boyhood,** that he was to be the salvation of the Grantleys in money ; nothing but **Ralph** Harnage's **tact could** have won his wayward mistress. **He was** obliged to make his advances carefully, practising a grave reserve, an **air of calm** indifference, which by **a** progress almost imperceptible he managed to change into **a** vague familiarity. Often his curses were not loud, **but** deep, in the face **of her** evident dislike ; **at times he** almost hated her, but the persistence **of the** man would not let **him resign her ;** it should **never be** said that he **was baffled** by a girl.

December was come again with its frosts and snows and iron rule, and the sun rose chill and watery to look upon Eunice's wedding-day. After weary months of solicitation, enfeebled with mourning for the departed and aching with anxiety for the living, she had given a weeping cold consent. She had been firm that nothing should induce her to marry until the two years were complete. And now twice twelve months had passed since the *Albatross* went down a charred and blackened wreck into the wide blue waters of the Pacific; and more than four years had gone by (a large piece out of a girl's life) since Harold went away to seek his· fortune; and yet his face was before her, his voice was in her ears as she made her lips utter the words that bind " until death do them part."

Oh! that there could be inspiration at

those supremest moments of our destiny, when recklessly unthinking we sign our own condemnation! A sound—an omen to startle us into vigilance, to arouse our slumbering senses which, alas! are not dead —which will awake in full vitality only to be tortured!

CHAPTER XIV.

Beware of desp'rate steps.   The darkest day,
Live till to-morrow, will have passed away.

 AM off presently to Chesney, and shall not be back till Thursday," said Mr. Harnage, stirring his coffee with a quick, irritable movement as he sat at breakfast opposite to his bride, in a dining-room furnished by Jackson and Graham regardless of expense, the walls adorned by costly paintings and old carved oak.

" Very well," replied Eunice.

" It ought not to be very well," snapped her husband, who thought he detected a certain degree of brightness in her assent. " If you were what a wife should be——"

" I should object to your going, or insist upon accompanying you ?"

" Exactly."

" Then let me go," said Eunice ; but spite her best efforts the request spoke little of the energy of desire.

" No ; stay where you are. I am going on business, and want no woman's rubbish."

" It is of no consequence," said his wife, listlessly. " If I had only Rip, I would as soon be in London as anywhere else."

" If that devilish bird had not had the taste to make his exit from this world with his master, I should certainly not have allowed him an entrance into a house of *mine*," said Mr. Harnage, who thought it no harm to acquaint his wife with his notions on subjects now they were one.

A fresh grief had come to Eunice. Lionel, for whose sake she partly made the sacrifice, had been killed not a month after her marriage by a fall from a dog-cart; and Rip, humped-up and disconsolate, had steadily refused food, and was one day found dead on Lionel's grave.

"Poor Rip! his brute constancy to dear Leo might have spared you the trouble of declining his society," said Eunice, and betraying symptoms of tears.

"*Constancy* is a virtue you affect, I know," sneered Ralph. "Crying again! Why, the woman's a living watering-pot; but I can't say I am revived by the process. If I am not to be permitted to speak in my own house without being swamped in tears, it will put the climax to my error."

"A climax, indeed!" said Eunice, ironically.

"I tell you what, Mrs. Harnage, my spirits are not sufficiently effervescing that I can stand a companion who has your sex's accomplishment of shedding tears at will in such perfection."

" Why did you marry me ?"

" Why indeed !" Being a man of the world the question did not embarrass him. " Since you ask me, it was merely to oblige your father, who, poor silly moth, had singed his wings on the Stock Exchange, until it was an act of charity to help him for the sake of old times."

" A pity," said Eunice, tersely ; " you could have assisted him without encumbering yourself with his daughter."

" True, *I might;* but the connexion gave an air of delicacy to the transaction." Having delivered himself of this sarcasm in the subdued tones peculiar to good breeding, Mr. Harnage took his fine person out of the room with much stateliness.

Life did not go smoothly with Eunice in her new estate : hers was a shadowy mockery of a marriage—as it must be when **any great** reality is dwindled into an **idle sham.** To the outward eye her affairs **were** flourishing; she had handsome houses, splendid equipages, obsequious servants: if her husband **were** a trifle neglectful it certainly did not form one **of** her griefs, for **to her** dismay, she found that she hailed his departure with relief—his coming with **a sinking heart**—that a dislike, unaccountable **to** her gentle nature, rather grew in spite of her struggles to stifle it. There was no sympathy between them. Thought and heart, habit and life must be as one, and in harmony to make a happy marriage ; there must be a mutual forbearance and toleration of weaknesses, and those candidates for wedded felicity, not dowered with this admirable patience, had best follow St. Paul's advice.

As the **great** father of the Church and

matrimony, **Martin** Luther says—" It is
an easy matter to take a wife, but to love
her without change, that is God's gift ; and
who can do this, let him thank God for it."
Mr. Harnage fell lamentably short in practice of this valuable precept; not six months
married to the woman he had striven hard
to make his wife, and he treated her with
indifference and scorn. Eunice discovered
that this courtly fair-seeming man could be
coarse and unkind, that when out of temper
he set no bounds to his remarks. She felt
some resentment, but little disappointment;
she had not hoped to find happiness, be-
lieving sincerely that joy for her was for
ever quenched in the burning of the
Albatross :—but she would have striven
after meek friendly relations with her
elderly spouse had she found anything in
his character that she could love or esteem.
Unhappily, every day brought some revela-

tion of his worldly cynical disposition to
shock her; while he chilled her gentle
advances by sneers at her—her people—her
lost love—her religion, until she was driven
to think of Harold with a more bitter regret,
a more intense sorrow.

Mr. Harnage had some grounds for complaint in his wife's apathy and melancholy.
Eunice had felt Lionel's death acutely; and
her father, broken down by this last blow,
was scarcely removed from imbecility, and
completely under the dominion of his foreign
wife : she had nothing she could now call a
home—no one to whom she could appeal
however sore her need; and the vague
terror that she was fettered and helpless in
the hands of this hard man changed her
whole nature ; and she brooded in listless
silence on her withered hopes, which lay
hidden in the secrecy of her thoughts like
wrecks beneath the sea.

Mr. Harnage's connubial sentiments were comprised in the two small words *in* and *out.* He had been *in* love with Eunice before marriage, and *out* of love three months after, and so thorough was the cure that not a vestige of tenderness remained to tell of the burnt-out fire. Love is difficult to define. Not love, the pure affection that seeks the good of its object, and not selfish gratification ; that love has only one face, a divine one—holy, tender, constant, wide-spreading, and covering a multitude of sins. But love, the passion, is a very different cherub, or demon—variously complexioned, owning endless vagaries and inconsistencies, and in its very essence evanescent.

Mr. Harnage's passion had too completely died out for him to be capable of jealousy, yet he resented Eunice's fidelity to the memory of a former lover, while her indifference to his frequent absences from home was another slight to his self-love. He might dine at his club night after night— even absent himself for days—she never complained. The idea of punishing her for this supineness by taking away carriages, fine dress, company, amusements, occurred to him, but was abandoned; she cared not for these luxuries—*ergo*, the zest for depriving her of them perforce expired. In the nineteenth century husbands of the humbler grades have the advantage; with the friendly ever-to-hand poker, and the familiar hob-nailed boot, they can and do make their helpmates feel the weight of their displeasure, and in very sensible form. Ralph Harnage had no weapon but his sarcasm that he could bring to bear, and such was his wife's deplorable insensibility, she seemed scarcely conscious of its use.

CHAPTER XV.

O terror ! what hath she perceived ?
O joy ! what doth she look on ?"

N a pleasant afternoon in April, a man drove up to the door of the Harnage town mansion in Eaton Square.

"Wait," said he, jumping lightly from the hansom; "I shall be only here a few minutes. I want to go on to the South-Western station.

"All right, yer honour." The cabman's face brightened, and he regarded his fare complacently as he stood on the door-steps, impatiently drumming his feet. The London cabby at all times gives a wise preference to male customers, knowing that

gentlemen are more usually well provided
with those easy wanderers, florins and half-
crowns.   This one looked specially promising.   Without being exactly foreign,
he bore a certain outlandish air which promised well for the chances of treble pay.
Evidently he had been roasted in the
tropics ; his naturally dark complexion was
bronzed almost to the tint of a Moor.
Above middle height and a good figure,
his face all women would regard with
pleasure, such dark expressive eyes !
though his thirty years must have been
busy to plough the deep furrows on the
broad low brow and around the mouth,
still beautiful with its firm curved lips.
There had been hurried attempts to adapt
his costume to the English régime ; his hat
was irreproachable, but his trousers were
baggy and queer, and his coat loose-fitting
and of a thin alpaca material, unknown

among the elect of the metropolis ; and his boots !—but we had best not glance at them ; for eyes used to Blobb's master-pieces the shock would be severe.

"Is Mr. Harnage at home ?" he asked of the young footman who at last answered the door (the butler was round the corner as usual).

Confused by his quick manner and strange accent, Jeames mistook the question, and imagining that his mistress was inquired for, replied in the affirmative.

" What name, sir ?"

But the half-articulated word was lost as the stranger sprung lightly up the stairs.

" Will you wait here, sir," and shutting the door, the servant withdrew to find Mrs. Harnage, leaving the visitor planted in the gorgeous front drawing-room. The young man glanced around admiringly, at the satin couches, the velvet curtains heavy with embroidery and softened by broad lace; at the Dresden and Sèvres china that ornamented the walls in costly profusion.

"Uncle Ralph always knew how to spend money *when* he had it," thought the visitor, with an amused smile; "but his taste has refined. I am in luck to catch him at home." He sank into a luxurious settee, and fell to contemplating Cottier's last chef-d'œuvre on the ceiling. "Don't like so much colour up there," he criticised; "it makes one feel as if one were in a box and the lid shut down. I wish he'd come!" and getting up, he took a few steps forward, advancing noiselessly on the thick carpet, and saw a vision that made his heart stand still. Then his pulse bounded, and a look of rapturous expectation dawned on his face.

The setting sun was shining forth in splendour, and its slanting beams fell full on a sofa at the end of the back drawing-room, the golden glory making a halo for the figure that lay there. Eunice looked exquisitely fair ; her complexion and bright brown hair thrown into strong relief by her black dress and the crimson velvet of the couch. Her eyes were closed, for without actually sleeping, she trembled on the borderland of dreams.

The supreme moments of our life generally come upon us in sober commonplace fashion. Eunice dozed peacefully, not a passing thought flitted across her slumber as warning that the moment was at hand which would for ever mar her peace of mind, make even calm resignation impossible ; nay more, lay her in the dust from which she would never rise.

" Eunice !" The glad exclamation burst

aloud from his lips, without pause or thought of preparation.

She started at once to her feet, petrified, as though she had been called by a spirit of another world, and stood breathless with amazement, her cheek pale as death, her eyes fixed and staring:—then a look of great joy came into them, as she saw that it was indeed he in the flesh.

"Harold! *not dead!*" she cried, with a faint shriek, and fell forward insensible into his arms.

He had not time to think—why had he found her here! he only caught the expression of bewilderment, almost fear—its quick transition to certainty and delight. A sensation of intense happiness thrilled him; this made amends for all: his long agony of patience bore fruit; the meeting he had dreamed of, and thought of, and prayed for, every day and night during

long years had **become a reality.** And in
a tumult of gladness, he strained **her to**
him, and bore her to the sofa she **had**
just quitted : his first emotions were **joy**
and wonder, but the wonder was swallowed
in the joy.

"The happiest day of **my** life," he
murmured. "Ah! *now I live:* **the present
is** for those who enjoy—the future for those
who suffer."

He kept his arms round her ; he **did** not
seek for remedies ; **her** spirit must come
back to answer **to his** love. **The black**
phantom of fear that **she** might have
ceased to care for him, which had long
oppressed him, vanished **in** the remembrance of her face at his sudden coming.
"She loved him still !—his faithful girl !"

He hung over her, covering her pale face
with kisses, studying every line : she was
adorably lovely, **and her mouth** bore as

11—2

rich a crimson as ever; but they had not taken care of her in his absence; she was thin and careworn. Perhaps she had sorrowed for him! A profound emotion stirred him. No matter, he had come back at last—no more black gowns and sober braided hair!—he would soon have the curls that had so bewitched him back again. She was only twenty-three; she had a long life before her, and please God, he would make it a happy one—atone for the sorrow she had suffered through him; their bliss would be the greater for their long trial; he was rich, and there was nothing to come between them now. He looked at her with a passionate affection as she lay on his shoulder; dear as the girl had been, he loved the thoughtful woman yet more.

She made an imperceptible movement.

"Eunice, sweet :—do not be alarmed. Speak to me."

She heaved a sigh ; she was coming back to her wretchedness, and a spasm of pain crossed her face.

"Eunice! my own. I have come back to you. Look at me—I want to see you."

Her eyes opened wide and full in a bewildered stare ; then she cowered closer to him, hiding her face.

"Wont you speak to me?" said he, beseechingly, and in a vague alarm, as he felt that she shivered. And—great Heaven ! was that—could it be—a *groan !*

Startled, he withdrew his supporting arm ; enlightenment flashed upon him, and quick as thought he seized her left hand, which hung down disregarded. Why was she here ?—in his uncle's house ! Why this despair ?—God !—could she be married !

"Let me die," she moaned. "Oh! that

I might die !" And her other hand went stealing up to hide her wretched shame. The first thing that caught his eye was his own ring, the half hoop of four pearls ; it had kept her true to him for four years ; again the promise had been kept to the ear and broken to the hope. It was the only ring she wore except the fatal circlet it guarded and half hid !

He could not grasp the fact in its full horrors ; he felt dizzy.

" *Married !*—to whom ?—to *my uncle?*"

A low heart-rending wail was her answer.

He withdrew from her stupefied, and staggered to his feet. His mind refused to recognise the full enormity of this marriage ; his heart beat violently, then seemed to stand still : he reeled, and only avoided falling by clutching at a table near.

All was a chaos of despair and misery.

More than once he swept his hand across his forehead, as if to clear away this amazing revelation. As for her, ages might have been counted on her heart in those minutes long in agony. They were silent. His faculties were concentrated in the immovable gaze with which he regarded her as she sat hiding her bowed face in both hands, and knowing in the darkness of her soul that all was lost. In those awful moments everything seemed to have slipped away from him—love, trust, faith; he suffered a moral earthquake; all was uprooted !—his belief in her love and purity, on which he had built in unshrinking confidence; the happy future he had pictured; all was crumbled away !—nothing remained but a hideous darkness, too black to contemplate.

Despair, like joy, takes no heed of time. He dashed himself on a chair. He saw it all !—it was all that cursed money! His uncle had become his heir, and had bought her. If she must insult his memory, why had she not at least chosen otherwise ?—his own uncle!

He got up like an automaton, and turned to leave the room without speaking; there was nothing—there could be nothing, to be said. She remained motionless, fear congealing her tears.

Eunice heard him going. Oh! that she could have died! If hearts would only break instead of suffer, she might have had her wish.

"Harold, speak to me. Don't go without a word; you will kill me." She stood up, pale and trembling, the sobs that had no relief in tears almost suffocating her.

He paused. What could she say—how defend herself?

"Harold—stay; hear me," her dry lips

scarcely able to articulate. " I thought you were dead—*dead*—oh ! so long ago—and they made me marry him."

" How ? Who *made* you ?" he asked, in fierce, hard scorn.

" All of them," she answered, distractedly. " I had no peace until I consented. It was that money you lent to father. Mr. Harnage wanted payment, and we had not got it to give, and I married him instead. I thought it did not signify much what became of me. Hate, despise me, Harold. I have been weak, mistaken, but forgive me, my dear, my only love," extending her arms piteously towards him. " I have never been untrue to you in thought. Pity me, for I am most wretched."

" I may pardon, but I *cannot* forget ;" and his lips were as granite. " I have preserved my faith in you pure and untouched, to find that you have vowed to love and

honour— *my uncle !* Any pure-souled girl
would have recoiled from such a desecration
of our love," said he, harshly. He cared
not for her pain ; an icy grasp seemed to
have seized his heart, paralysing all feeling.
His dangers, his trials, his love-dreams, his
longings after happiness were ended, they
had come to this !—and it was her hand
that pierced him : there was the pain, for

> To be wroth with one we love,
> Doth work like madness in the brain.

Her head drooped low in her self-abase-
ment. What had she done ? She had
murdered his happiness as well as her own ;
she was the wickedest woman in creation.

"Why did you never write, never tell
me that you were saved ?" she asked,
passionately. " I only married five months
ago."

"I could not write. But I forget, you
know nothing. I floated away on a spar,
and was picked up by some natives, and

taken to their island; and I have lived there alone with only savages for companions ever since, hoping against hope that a ship would pass and bring me home. The belief in your faithfulness alone kept me from going mad." He came nearer, and stood over her like an avenging spirit, drawing his breath in quick short pants. " And I have come back *for this !* Who shall restore my lost hope—who give me back the brightness you have destroyed ? My soul has cherished but one dream ; your shadow has been always on my heart. On the pale sea I have traced your form ; in the hot stifling night, your spirit has come at my call to give me patience and renew my hope.—And *for this !* It is too much."

She shrunk, withering sensibly like a flower under his scorching words and dry burning eyes.

Again he turned to leave the house.

"Where are you going, Harold?" she asked, humbly.

"I am going home to burn my idol," said he, bitterly.

"Stay! only hear me, Harold, dear Harold. I am not all to blame. I, too, have suffered. I would not believe that you were dead. I refused to think heaven could be so cruel. For a whole year I expected and watched for you. And then I gave up hoping, and put on this," touching her dress. "I have never forgotten you, or ceased to grieve. See! I have worn your ring and none other, night and day, since you put it on."

He forgave her from that moment, for there was truth in her wild sad accents. His face softened and he made a step nearer.

"*None other*, Eunice?" said he, reproachfully. "Oh! why did you do it?" his voice full of anguish.

"Forgive me, Harold," stretching her arms towards him. "You told me that he had been good and kind to you. Oh! I am the most unhappy woman breathing!" her hands dropped nervelessly by her side, and big tears rolled down her pale face.

"What would you have me do, Eunice?" his voice very troubled.

She went forward and knelt to him to make her prayer. "Say, 'Eunice, I forgive you.'"

He raised her and took her in his arms: hideous sin or not he must comfort his poor stricken girl, and then he would go away and never put himself in the temptation of seeing her again.

They sat together, and he stroked her hair and wiped her tears with his own handkerchief: soon she looked at him, an ineffable joy in her soft hazel eyes, and a smile crept round the mouth.

" Why do you smile, Eunice ? *How can you ?*"

" Because I am so glad."

" *So glad !*"

" Yes, I am so glad you are alive. I have had such dreams, that you were lying at the bottom of the sea, surrounded by loathsome creatures. But you have a long and happy life before you"—a prophetic, far-seeing look in her eyes.

" *Happy*—without you ?"

" This house is yours, is it not ?" said she, slowly ; " and—everything ?"

He nodded. " I suppose so."

" I want to ask you something."

" What is it ?"

" Will you give me a cottage—anywhere —where I can hide myself till I die ? I can't go home !" she shivered. " Lady Grantley is cruel; she made me marry him. I should not mind being indebted to you for a home."

" This is your home; do you think I would take anything from you ?"—he could scarcely command his voice to speak.

" As you please," she answered, meekly.

" *He* is kind to you, is he not ?" asked Harold, suddenly.

" I do not think he is—not since he found that I did not like him. He is hard ; he is not a good man, though he is your uncle," she continued, hurriedly. " But that is *nothing.* I prefer that he should not like me."

Harold felt that he could not bear it much longer. The demon of revenge was knocking at his breast, and made him feel murderous.

" When do you expect him home ?"

" I do not know ; perhaps this evening. He is a great deal away at his country house."

" I will come in the morning, and see him." Harold rose to go, a saddened man, twenty years older than when he entered the room.

"And you are sure that you forgive me, Harold?" she said, wistfully.

"As I hope to be forgiven, my poor darling. You are more sinned against than sinning."

CHAPTER XVI.

Three things a wise man will not trust,
The wind, the sunshine of an April day,
And woman's plighted faith.

AROLD, still dazed by the blow that had fallen on him, passed out into the placid every-day life. He walked on swiftly, oblivious of the ill-used cabman, who considered that an hour's waiting at theatre and dinner-going time rather a strong order. Brought to bay by the energetic — "Heighs !" and "Look ye 'ere, sirs," Harold gave the driver a half sovereign.

"Hain't yer honour going to the Waterloo Station ?"

Harold sighed, a sigh that was more

nearly a groan, as if he would remove some crushing weight from his chest.

" No, thank you ; no need."

Nothing was to be gained by going to Grantley ; he had found his lady-love nearer and more easily than he expected.

He stalked on, scarce knowing whither he went. A boy came up and begged of him persistently. Harold threw him a shilling, and the child dashed off without thanks, fearful perhaps that the gift might be recalled, or in a hurry of delight to examine in some secluded corner the extent to which he had been so unexpectedly enriched.

" I would rather be that barefooted outcast," thought Harold, bitterly. A darkness of night was upon him, the castle he had erected with such fond care was laid prostrate, and he stood desolate among its ruins. She had placed an insurmountable barrier **between them, which not even** Death could destroy ; she was utterly **lost** to him ; in honour he must **avoid her as he** would a pestilence.

In any overwhelming grief or disappointment, the yearning **desire of** the **human** mind **is for complete annihilation ; it is as** if rest, oblivion **from** trials too heavy **to be** borne, must **be** purchased **at any cost.** Had a pistol been to his hand, Harold would have been sorely tempted **to put it** to his heart, and so far as we know ended its aching for ever. But where life is more terrible than death, **to** dare to live **becomes the truest courage. His anger** against Eunice had already **died out ; revenge he** could not feel—would he revenge mistake and unhappiness ? **No, his life would** still have an object ; he would watch **over and** protect her from this robber—*her husband !*

For while deepest **pity and** solicitude

12—2

for her filled him, these tender feelings merged in consuming rage and hate as he remembered Ralph Harnage ; and the desire for vengeance burned within him like a fire, gathering fierceness, and unfolding itself into definite schemes as he pondered in passionate resentment on his wrongs.

What could he do ?—how much were they in Ralph's power ?—did their whole capacity for suffering come within the hellish range of his enemy ?

An unpleasant gleaming light shot into his dark eyes for answer ;—he touched his pocket significantly. He would have him *there.* This man, the perfection of baseness, impenitent as a snake, remorseless as a tiger, had one vulnerable point ; and he should find some one pitiless as himself.

Eunice lay in a heap on the floor, too overcome by her wretchedness to care to move; sunk in a stupor, she forgot the flight of time. A servant peeped in, and discreetly withdrew unnoticed, to recount to Mam'selle Blanche the strange sight he had witnessed of Mrs. Harnage grovelling on the floor of her gilded drawing-room, and "talking to herself hawful." At first Eunice was stunned into numbness.—But this stage never lasts ; the mind, active and reasoning, will reassert its powers—inquiring into and recognising its unhappiness. She silently brooded on the past ; then, frenzied at the present—at what was to come, she broke into disordered speech. For her deplorable case there was no relief but—despair ; no remedy—but death. "Oh! let me die !—let me die !" she moaned again and again.

She execrated her insensate folly ; this marriage had been so unnecessary, so superfluous !—Lionel dead, her father in his imbecile state almost dead to his em-

barrassments, the sacrifice made, only evil
had come of it. Her own act had separated
them for ever, and not all the tears she
could shed might wipe away the remembrance of her unnatural conduct. Self-
reproach, that keenest tormentor, stabbed
her ; yet were her sobs of anguish mingled
with tumultuous bursts of gladness that
he lived ! His return to the world in
which she had ceased to hope to see him,
while it entailed endless wretchedness, yet
brought a great joy.

" Madame est servie.—Madame n'a pas
fait sa toilette ce soir," said the smart
French lady's-maid, driven to the verge of
endurance by her mistress's prolonged
neglect of the two most important duties
in life.

Eunice rose pale and chill, and staggered
from the room—she must try to hide her
heavy cross.

CHAPTER XVII.

Sustain me in this trial, sweet patience, and lock up the memory that fills the vessels of my heart with gall, and stamps on shame the colour of revenge.

RALPH HARNAGE'S state of mind that night was not conducive to repose. Man is a complicated animal; few of the species are absolutely good; still fewer, be it said, for the honour of poor human nature, are altogether evil:—in the noblest the cloven foot will peep out—for the basest some excuse may be found.

Ralph Harnage, to do him justice, was horrified—shocked at his nephew's re-appearance; even his iron composure and self-control were overthrown by this unlooked-for event. He really liked Harold, and had it not been for his unlucky appropriation of Eunice, he could even—or he thought he could—have welcomed him home, and yielded him his inheritance without a pang. But however nepotic one's tendencies, it is trying to have the most dearly loved relative resurrectionized after over two years supposed adieu to earthly scenes; peculiarly so in this instance—a man (no longer a boy to be put off with excuses) claiming the fortune he had securely deemed his own; and worse still, demanding with eyes of fire and white lips his promised wife. He had gathered already so much in his interview with Eunice, that Harold was faithful, inconveniently faithful, to his love.

And she!—how she glared at him!—and told him never to come into her sight again. She looked quite dangerous, with her small, white face and gleaming eyes. He only wished to Heaven! (or rather his adjurations were directed to a hotter situation) that he had left the puling milk-and-water chit alone: he had lived in a shower-bath of her tears, and his naturally fine spirits had been unnaturally depressed since the ill-omened day of their union.

Mr. Harnage, more than once, in the course of his ceaseless ramble up and down his room, contemplated the feasibility of an immediate flight to the Continent, leaving Harold master of the field, without giving himself the opportunity of uttering a word of defence or explanation. But Ralph, not being a shy or timid man, resolved to stand his ground: there was much to be said in extenuation for his offence, and natural affection for one who had been in the place of a father to him, must also, he reflected, plead his cause powerfully with Harold.

These consolatory notions, though sufficiently calming to procure him an hour's feverish repose, availed him little when he found himself face to face with his nephew next morning in the solitude of the correctly furnished library. He stood before the man who had risen to confront and confound him, "a spirit from the vasty deep," as in the presence of a wraith; his face blanched and he seemed to become suddenly withered and aged—deep lines in his forehoad and a drooping jaw. His eyes were cast down—he could not face the intense light that burned in Harold's; even a heart hardened by systematic selfishness shrunk before the deserved hatred which glowed in that concentrated look of passion.

Harold rejected his uncle's proffered hand

in cold scorn, though **he** could **have** wept,
or gnashed his teeth in **fruitless** rage.

If the man had looked winsome, **if** he
could have pleaded the headlong wanton-
ness of youth, Harold felt that **he** might
have had pity, he might almost have **for-**
given him ; but this was **the** deliberate
purpose **of a** hoary sinner to attain **his**
wicked end. He breathed vengeance and
fury, yet outwardly he remained calm, self-
possessed. **He** schooled **himself**—" **I will**
be stern as reason, pitiless as justice ; **he**
shall have *justice !* This man has taken **my**
Eunice, my own, **my angel !** and **he does**
not even love her, or care for her happiness !" And Harold's hands clenched at
the thought, his eyes flashed, and **the veins**
of his brow swelled almost to bursting ; he
could have slain him where he stood, and
felt it *justice !*—for had **he** not robbed him
of more than life—his heart's dearest **trea-**

sure? he had dashed away the full cup of happiness from his parched lips. The deed was done, past recal. Love and hope were gone for ever! Now to business.

He remembered the miser—his spoiled life; his mother wooed from another only to be neglected; his Eunice betrayed and wretched; and his heart was as ice, and his reproaches sharp arrows that did not miss their mark—they shot home. The culprit cowered beneath the fiery shower of words; his character was revealed to himself in its native blackness; he could not palliate his conduct.

"You have raised the devil, and must face the devil; but at least you are spared the task of giving the devil his due just yet," said Harold, sneeringly. "You will only have to refund all that you have appropriated of mine; you must be aware that you are the last man on earth Matthew

Harnage intended should enjoy a penny of his money."

" What is done cannot be recalled," said Ralph, gloomily. " I have been much to blame, but the mischief is not irreparable. I will go away ; it will avoid disturbance."

" You will be wise."

Mr. Harnage regarded his nephew anxiously. " I see how you are bound up in Eunice," he went on diffidently. " You have the prior claim. When she told me last evening of your return, she said that she hated me—she could not endure the sight of me. She has been pining away ever since your disappearance ; and it's my belief she's dying for you."

Mr. Harnage paused. " Are you attending to me ? I only see your back."

" I hear you," said Harold, laconically. Mr. Harnage paused again. Harold still

looked towards the window, his hands
thrust deep down in his pockets. Mr.
Harnage went on in desperation, "Take
her, and go abroad. Absent yourself for a
few months; leave the affair ambiguous,
and it will come right."

Harold turned suddenly and gazed at his
uncle steadfastly.

"You mean that you would divorce her
to oblige me?" said he, quietly.

Mr. Harnage nodded—an uneasy nod.
Harold's hands released from his pockets
were clenched in an unpleasantly suggestive manner, as though fain to strike
some one.

"You know that I could not marry her!"
Harold burst out. "And you counsel me
to bring disgrace and ruin on the woman I
love better than my life!" His tones were
raised: and he walked across the room;
then coming and standing close to his

uncle for the **first time, he** hissed between his teeth—"I believe that **you are** the devil in man's shape **to tempt** me **thus**— to propose such a bargain. But that **is** your way," he continued, with a sudden gnashing fierceness. "You have bought my wife with my own money, and having **sold** her **body, you** would complete **your** work by selling her soul. **You are a** demon ! but *I will not listen* **to** *you !* I no longer wonder there **be souls** weak **or** strong enough to believe in magic and the **power** of fiends—that she could have sunk **so** **low as to** become *your wife !"*

His uncle's wickedness **was** such, Harold marvelled that horns did not sprout from his forehead and flames issue **from his** mouth.

Harold's wrath **was** fearfully scathing, the more so that **he** had it under control.

Ralph's **face was dyed** with the dusky

red of shame. The contrast between the two men was great; the one cowered like a beaten hound, his grey hairs only adding to his degradation, while Harold threw his head aloft, and with kindled eyes had all the majesty of innocence and right. It is when the blaze of passion light's up a man's nature that we see the impress clearly, we honour in him the sign of a celestial origin, or we weep the dishonour of a demi-god.

This contempt was in Ralph Harnage's opinion hard and undeserved. He walked according to his lights, and to him virtue was an abstraction, and honour merely a name: he considered morality another term for cant; that it depended upon circumstances, and was framed by men only to guard their own convenience. The man was not without spirit, and he would like to have turned and defied his accuser, but he knew Harold's power; he knew that he had not a farthing he could call his own, and **he** felt too old **and** enervated by his **late** prosperity to begin the battle for bread all over again. This consideration **kept** his tone servile. Eunice at least was his property, his one trump card, and **he** must play her to the best advantage.

" I am only anxious to meet your **views** in every way. Show me how I can make reparation. **If** by any sacrifice—I **do not** wish to annoy Eunice."

"No fear; you shall **not** trouble *her*," replied Harold, coldly. " **I have an** argument you will not despise—*self-interest.* This is our last meeting—God willing, I will never see you again!—all **necessary** business can be transacted through **my** lawyer. **I** request you to leave England at once : you **will receive four** hundred pounds a year, paid **quarterly at your foreign abode.** Should you infringe **the** conditions, or attempt in any way to molest your wife by letters or otherwise, you will be immediately sued for the whole back funds that you have enjoyed for the last two years, in which case a debtor's prison will release her effectually from your un-wished-for presence."

Impotent rage flashed into Mr. Harnage's night-black eyes. How he hated Eunice, the innocent cause of his humiliation!

"These are hard terms. I think you outstep your——"

"I know my legal rights," interrupted his nephew, in icy contempt; "and if driven to it, shall not hesitate to enforce them. I have come back to watch over her: though I cannot be her husband, I will be a brother, to protect her from further wrong." And he left the room without bestowing another glance on the wretched man.

Eunice waiting and listening in her grand dining-room, felt his approach without seeing it; his feet trod upon her heart when as yet their sound was unheard. She waited in vain; he passed on—the front-door closed. He had gone without seeking to see her! How she longed for death! In her desolation, Death was her only possible friend—the only help she had the right to long for.

13—2

CHAPTER XVIII.

Les vives couleurs s'effacent, elle languit, elle se desèche, et sa belle tête se penche, ne pouvent plus se soutenir.—FENELON.

OPELESS and miserable as was the state of affairs, the great arranger, Time, in the course of some days, shook even these perturbed atoms into some degree of order.

Mr. Harnage, after having thoroughly ascertained the state of the home barometer, being, moreover, a gentleman of some astuteness, who knew when he held the trump cards, and when he did not, had betaken himself to the German baths, at the advice of his doctor, he having been previously advised by the family lawyer

that Harold's was no vain boast ; that his
nephew *could* and *would* act upon his
threat, if the debtor refused to disappear.
Ralph now disliked his wife so heartily,
that it was an additional motive for the
exile, that he would be relieved from
seeing her wretched little white face.
Why had he ever meddled with her ?
There was never a mischief that a woman
was not at the bottom of it.

Thus a strange state of things came to
pass. Eunice lived alone in the stately
mansion, that still owned her as mistress ;
and it was her one comfort, that Mr.
Harnage had relieved her of his presence.
He took no formal farewell, and she knew
not when he might return, for Harold had
told her nothing, he left everything to be
inferred ; nor did she see him again for
more than a fortnight after their first
meeting. She wondered and waited—the

usual rôle of womankind—and, a prey to
sickening sensations of doubt and dis-
tracting regret, she each day grew more
wan and miserable. To know he breathed
the same air, was so near, and yet never
came to see her, wore her with a perpetual
fretting. She did not expect much, but
he need not show so plainly that he had
ceased to care for her.

He was staying away, poor fellow!—
trying to school himself for their new
position. His slumbering virtue was
roused and strengthened by his uncle's
base hints,—and he would not see her
again until he had endued his mind with
the fact that she could never be anything
more to him than a dear friend. And he,
too, had tormenting doubts whether he
had been justified in sending away his
uncle; would it not place her in an
equivocal position? But she had said that

she *could not* live with Ralph. — Besides, his fierce desire for retaliation must have vent ; and it satisfied him somewhat that this robber should be despoiled of his ill-gotten property.

At last he came. He looked very handsome—much more so, Eunice thought, than even in the old days. There was a manliness in his bronzed face, a self-reliance in his manner, and a decision in his speech, which were in her opinion eminently becoming ; and not Lord Errington's self could have been habited in more irreproachable costume. If he wished to cure Eunice, the wish did not take the form of making himself personally unacceptable.

" Not gone out this fine afternoon ?" said Harold, lightly, meeting her with a handshake, and apparently not noticing the deep flush that for a minute hid the ravages of care.

"I did not want to go out. I thought you might call," she answered, faintly.

"I have been very busy," said he, sitting down at the impartial distance usually assumed by a morning caller. "I am just back from Chesney; it is a beautiful place. London looks very hard and un-interesting after its verdant glades."

Eunice could scarcely speak. It was evidently his pleasure that they should be mere friends, and she bowed to it meekly.

"Then you will not be in town long?"

"That depends. I suppose I must stay a short time. At Rome one must do as the Romans do; one can't cut the season altogether. I met Mostyn this morning, and he asked me to dine at his club. I accepted for 'Auld lang syne.'"

The ready tears started to Eunice's eyes.

"You have told me nothing about poor Lionel," he went on, in a kinder voice; "it must have been a sad blow to you, and to your father."

"It was indeed," said she in stifled tones.

"And Rip—he would be a mourner, I am sure?"

"Poor Rip! he soon died. He refused food, and, some days afterwards, he was found dead on Lionel's grave."

"I always said Rip's disposition was whiter than his coat. This gentleman in black developed, then, the rare virtue—*constancy.* I give him all praise; we should think highly of unattainable virtues."

His chilling look and harsh words were hard to bear; but she only cast an imploring glance at him, with pretty deprecating humility in her lovely eyes.

"Will you tell me — Harold" — she hesitated over the name; he was so cold and unbending, she feared to say it— "how you were saved? I have heard so little yet."

"It was a dreadful time. I never willingly recal it."

"But *tell me*," said she, eagerly. "Tell me all—every particular."

He stooped his head, and put up his hand before his face.

"Not if it is too painful," she continued, gently.

"No, no," said he, with an effort. "I will tell you—you have a right to hear; but the memories are all sad. When I think of my exultant joy that day—it was the last day of my youth!—the clouds have darkened and closed in around me hopelessly ever since.

"We had been five days at sea, and

were making way bravely. The sun looked down from a cloudless sky with too much fervour to be altogether pleasant; the heat being so great that forenoon, it made the water rise in curling vapours; while birds hovered overhead, and darted through the rigging as we cut the waves with a merry rushing sound, and coming near, allowed the sailors to catch them, as if yielding to a fatality. Some said it showed that we were near land; one an old seaman, shook his head, muttering, 'they were ill-omed varmin, that always accompanied a doomed ship.' Towards sunset a breeze sprung up, which freshened into a stiff wind, and tempered the intolerable heat. It was an hour from sundown; I had gone to my cabin, and was in my hammock, when I heard a low, growling sound, which mingled with, and yet was quite distinct from the regular drumming of the paddle-wheels ; and then a sudden wild cry—'*Fire! Fire!*—the ship's on fire !' The yell that followed was appalling ; all knew the significance of that cry. I ran up on deck, where the confusion had already become indescribable. Men, pale as ashes, hurried hither and thither at the direction of the officers, impeded by the panic-struck passengers, and to the accompaniment of the shrieks and groans of the women and children. ' The fire is raging in the stowage hold,' said the first mate to me ; ' a miracle only can save us. God only knows how it originated.'

" The engines had been stopped, and the crew were already at the pumps ; but the anarchy that had set in with the danger prevented any organized means of trying to check the flames, though all the sailors, and many of the passengers, did their best. I worked with desperation, for to get the fire under **was** clearly the only hope. The wind had become our deadliest enemy; it fanned the fire, now bursting up in great tongues of flame; and the smoke was so dense, that it wrapped **and half** blinded the men at the pumps, **as** we continued to pour volumes of water **down** the hold. Spite of everything, the fire gathered **in** intensity, and the air was filled with the roar of the flames (overpowering the growling of the engines, which had seemed to mock our efforts like a prisoned fiend), and hissing under the water, they leaped defiantly upwards, encircling in their fatal bands, masts, shrouds, and sails.

The uselessness of our toil was apparent : already we had lost two boats. And the confusion and hideous outcry in the face of the helpless death before us!—persons in every attitude of frenzy; none quiescent, none resigned. The remaining four boats had been guarded by the captain's orders: but any attempt at further discipline was useless. The boats were rushed at as the only means of salvation, and torn down by frantic hands, were crowded to excess before they touched the water. One man, an invalid, and supposed to be in a dying state, in the excitement of this fresh and nearer view of death, managed to push and struggle into the boat despite the mortal paleness on his forehead. Maddened by fear, many were like raging animals. In vain the captain entreated and commanded; amid shrieks and groans the boats filled with teeming life until they became floating biers. One capsized before it was well loosed from its davits. Another had sheered off, but went down at the very moment a woman clutched at the side of the already

overloaded boat, strewing the sea with unfortunate creatures—some grasping the
crackling bulwarks — some disappearing
with arms thrown high, catching convulsively at air. None attempted a rescue.
Not the most fearful scene in Dante's
imagined Inferno equals the horrors I then
saw. Sometimes during the night I fancy,
even now, that I hear the rush of waters,
and people floating by clinging to spars and
calling for assistance."

Harold covered his face with both hands.
Eunice sat listening, pale and mute, her
eyes distended with a painful eagerness in
his recital.

" But the other boats ?" she asked, in
awe-stricken tones.

" Two got off, labouring heavily, the keels
so deep in the water that a rough wave,
another man, and they too must have gone
to the bottom.—And the despair of those

left behind! But the appalling scene could not last much longer : the burning cordage and blackened canvas fell in showers on the deck, driving the few left on board into the tantalizing waves. Men and women who could not swim a stroke jumped over knowingly, choosing the speediest solution of the horrors surrounding them."

"But you were in the boat ?"

"No—not that my life was not dear to me as to any struggling mortal there."

"But *you*—what did you do ?" asked Eunice, her whole soul in the question, and pale as marble.

"Oh ! I had been very selfish," he replied, with a sad smile. "Love made me cunning, and at the first alarm, I managed to secure a life-belt ; and you shall hear what a friend it proved to me. Only the captain, a passenger, and myself remained on deck, and I lashed myself to a large piece of spar, my companions following my example. I jumped into the sea : its coolness revived me, and I struck out as well as I could."

" Yes, yes, go on."

" Soon I rested on the spar, content to husband my strength, and praying fervently the tide might carry me to shore. The calamity had come too suddenly to ascertain our whereabouts, but it was possible we were near land ; or I might be seen by a ship. Both forlorn hopes ; but the drowning wretch is fain to catch at straws of comfort. It was an awful feeling of desolation alone on the ocean, and night coming on. The wind moderated ; and the sun set gorgeously, dressing the deep· blue sky in a shadowy embroidered garment of opalescent clouds ; the waves rippled on burying many a stout heart under their deceitful surface ; and the breeze swept balmily, breathing fresh life into my weary limbs. Then of a sudden, the burning sea of light overhead darkened, and at the same moment, the lurid glow of the *Albatross* subsided into black columns of smoke, that floated away, unheeded messengers of our calamity. Where was the ship—the crew? —the bitterness of death was past; all was tranquil as the grave. I rested my head on the spar, making no attempt to direct my course. I knew the tide was my master, and would carry me further and faster than my strongest efforts. After a time, the noise of the water boomed and buzzed in my ears, and parti-coloured rays of light flashed across my sight. I could scarce breathe; the pulses of my brain throbbed as if they would burst. A stupor of exhaustion, which I thought the beginning of death, came over me; my eyes, which had gazed on the sky as it appeared to me for an interminable period, saw it no more ; the agony of the present no longer lived for me."

" *Poor, poor* Harold !" ejaculated Eunice, in deepest, tenderest pity.

" The next thing I recollect is a copper-coloured face with beetling brows and black matted hair bending over me. I had been picked up by some natives of an island near, who were out fishing in a canoe of the rudest manufacture. Surrounded by those black faces, with their gleaming teeth, and burning eyes glaring into mine, I thought they were devils—that the dissolution of body and soul had come, and that I must in truth have reached the infernal regions. I had been for hours insensible, and felt weak and dizzy. My deliverers seemed to be Magyars, and did not understand the few words of Hindostanee I had learned in Ceylon. I tried by signs to interest them in my companions' fate : it was hopeless to make any impression on their humanity ; they held on their way ; and in time we landed. I thrilled with joy as I put foot on ground ; intense gratitude that I had escaped death to see you again filled me."

He paused and looked dreamily at her. She sat motionless, unconscious of his gaze, her eyes alone, reflecting the interest of his narrative, gave indications of life. He resumed with a sigh—" But how little did I foresee the weary length of waiting that I should have to endure. For two years I existed there, leading a savage life, eating out my heart in vain attempts to leave the island. No vessel ever touched there as far as I could hear.

" How dreadful !" said Eunice, " and I did not know—I only felt that you lived."

" You can imagine, Eunice, what I suffered ; the anguish of long waiting ; the

horrors of constantly striving to leave the
island that had become a loathsome prison,
which, though teeming with life, was a
vast tomb for me. I left Ceylon with
buoyant feelings, full of enthusiastic anticipations of love, friendship, generosity; with
a multitude of senses and passions all
promising happiness in their pursuit and
gratification. Well! I had time to cool
down from these youthful imaginings.
The natives used to think me mad because
I passed my days on the highest ground
hoisting my poor signals, and looking for
rescue that never came. No sail ever
blessed my sight; we were out of the track
of vessels. Once I stole a canoe and went
off in the night, able to bear the suspense
no longer; but they followed me, and
managing their boat better, overtook and
brought me back. After that I was strictly
watched and cruelly treated; most likely

they would have killed me had I looked a worthier target to expend their arrows upon ; as it was they were only contemptuous of the forlorn creature who had been cast upon their mercies."

" Were there any women on the island?"

" Numbers, for, not in conformity with Indian practice, the fair, or rather whity-brown portion of the community are allowed to live. They were my best friends. The women are slaves to their husbands, and what is wonderful, are content with their lot. It will probably be long before the emancipation of the sex is to be looked for among the Magyars. We lived principally on fish and roots, and to this Pythagorean diet I attribute the peaceable disposition of these dark descendants of Ham. After awhile I earned their respect by the skill with which I learned to use their weapons, and obtained

their goodwill by pursuing English modes
of treatment in their illnesses ; but my one
idea through it all was to get away. I
thought of nothing else night and day. At
length, despairing of a ship coming to my
rescue, and having crept in favour with the
chief, I procured materials and began to
build a boat, one stronger and more calcu-
lated to bear the elements than their frail
canoes. The chief pitying my eagerness,
made his people help me, and sped me on
my enterprise with advice and provisions.
All was ready, and I prepared to depart,
though I indulged small hopes of ever
getting to England. Desperation and the
thought of you alone made me dare the
waste of waters in a rough, ill-made boat
which a single wave might upset. I started
in a calm, and it frightened me to see what
a little way I made. Then the longed for
breeze sprung up, and I set my tiny sail.

My courage rose. I had christened my sail 'Eunice' because it was white and pure."

Eunice shivered, and hid her face in her hands.

"I looked upon it as a good omen that it already served me well, and I steered my course, as well as I could make it out by the compass I had made, for the track of ships. Four days I sailed on, and then I saw a steamer. Great God! what were my emotions at the sight! I shrieked and shouted and waved a dead branch like a maniac. They took no notice, and passed gallantly on their way, leaving a poor struggling creature to his despair. The torture of that disappointment! After awhile I forgot my torments in sleep—a sweet sleep. I dreamed that I was with you, that you had rescued me, and woke to find that I had been observed by a small

Dutch vessel. They had seen my sail, and bearing down, perceived me, and soon had me on board. But," with a quick change of tone, " you must be tired of listening to my story. I have made it longer than I intended."

" Tired," said she, reproachfully. " But how did you get home? how came you here—to this house ?"

" That is very simple and easily told. The Dutchmen were very kind, and when near Madeira transferred their waif and stray to a homeward bound British vessel, where I received every attention. They fed and clothed me, for civilized possessions I had none ; and they provided me with money for my journey to London. I went straight to Messrs. Ward and Roberts. It was the surest means to get news of my uncle, and through him, tidings of you. I heard that he had succeeded to my property—had of course cut the City concern, and lived in Eaton Square. I waited for no more, and came on here at once. You know the rest."

He got up and walked to the window, and was apparently engrossed in the amusement afforded by the square—a promising game of lawn tennis enacted by some smartly dressed damsels in large Rubens hats.

"You have some pretty neighbours," he remarked, in a voice of interest. "Do you know who they are?"

"No," she replied, and her heart died within her at this trifling. "They will not be my neighbours long."

"How? why?" quickly turning to her.

"Because—because," trying to speak firmly in spite of a choking sob, "I cannot stay here. I have no right to do so—no claim upon you."

"Eunice, will you stay, if I ask it of you, as the *one* thing you can do for me— to make me—to give me pleasure?" said he, earnestly.

"It shall be as you wish. But you will come and see me sometimes, will you not?" said she, gazing up at him beseechingly.

"I will, Eunice, my——" He checked abruptly forbidden words that rose to his lips. "I must go now. Good-bye, and take care of yourself."

"And you will come again soon?" she persisted, wistfully.

"I have to go down to Chesney again. Better not expect me till you see me."

And with a mere handshake they parted.

CHAPTER XIX.

Of all affliction taught a lover yet,
'Tis sure the hardest science to forget.

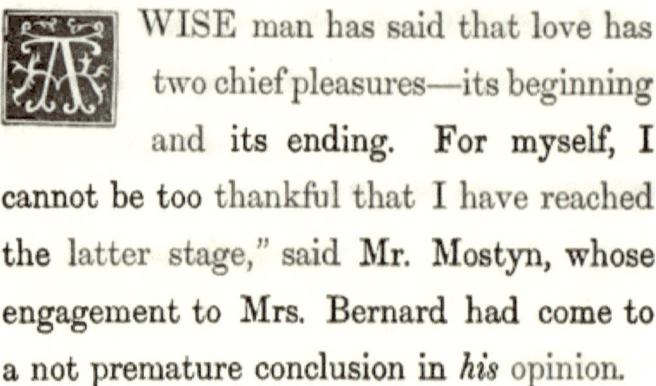 WISE man has said that love has two chief pleasures—its beginning and its ending. For myself, I cannot be too thankful that I have reached the latter stage," said Mr. Mostyn, whose engagement to Mrs. Bernard had come to a not premature conclusion in *his* opinion.

Mr. Mostyn had looked up Harold Harnage most determinately, impelled not so much by that liberality of sentiment which commonly, "like the world, its ready visit pays where fortune smiles," as by a similarity which he fancied to exist be-tween his own and Harold's blighted love-prospects. (The widow had thrown him over at the last moment in favour of a cousin in shameful fashion, though he never failed to profess himself grateful for the escape.)

"Yes, there is an unappreciated treasure of affection in this breast," said Mr. Mostyn, modestly, and tapping his protuberant shirt-front. "Such is the irony of fate—the perpetual contrast between our nature and destiny—the tenderness that, prodigal-like, I would have lavished upon *one*, finds now an outpouring in benevolence to my fellow-creatures. You could not have come" (he had insisted on finding his way into our hero's chambers) "to a man who knows better how to parry the cruel strokes of fate. *I* have felt *them all*."

Again he attacked his shirt-front, but with greater energy.

"I am busy," said Harold. "I am

going to run down to Chesney this afternoon."

" Alone ?"

" Alone."

" A mistake. Eschew solitude, man," said Mostyn, continuing his well-meant attempts to cheer his moody companion. " You have had too much of it already ; better see life ; boxed up in that infernal hole of an island you are as verdant as if you had dropped from one of the Cape Verdes ! See life — that is my prescription." It was one Mostyn acted upon ; he had done nothing else, and had thriven and grown fat on it ; no wonder he recommended it. " My dear fellow, no one can pity you more sincerely than F. M. Why, you've been dead to the world so long that you're like a ghost among the living. By Jove ! you can enter into the sensations of Robinson Crusoe !"

"*I can;* the veriest bore would then have relieved me by his presence. I do my best," Harold went on, thinking his last remark rather pointed. "Time is my bitterest enemy, and it is naturally my chief anxiety to kill him. I select the ordinary means that present themselves—amusements, follies."

"That is a morbid way of putting it," said Mostyn, waggling his head in disapproval. "My friend, I am sorry for you. Take my advice, and fly over Europe ; it is the only thing to do in these cases."

Harold's dark eyes shot inexpressible disdain.

"*What cases ?*"

"Don't mind me," answered his visitor, soothingly. "I am behind the scenes ; besides, I have been through it all. But when you have come to my age, you will be more philosophical ; you will know that one woman is pretty much the same as another. Now there is that Mrs. Wodehouse —(Miss Danecourt, you know)—a widow, and all her money settled on herself."

" Did her marriage turn out well ?"

" Ill—very ill—husband a victim to D. T. —suicide out of the top floor front window, and so forth."

" But the lady of the dollars is equally in the condition of Hecuba. What's she to us, or we to her, that we should weep for her ?" said Harold, bitterly.

" The Verschoyles say that she is *seriously épris* with you," said Mostyn, resolved to bring his friend down to more commonplace and common-sense views. She cherishes a romantic admiration for your feat in saving her brother from the train."

" *Seriously,* I am much flattered."

" You must either travel or marry," said Mostyn, with a degree of contemplation that was assisted by his cigar. "*I* should choose the former, **as** the safer and **plea-santer** alternative ; **but** perhaps *you* have had enough in that line for the present."

" I think I have."

" And Mrs. Wodehouse **is** *the* catch **of** the season, and ready to drop **into** your mouth **if you will but open it** seasonably. Your advantages are so great—a fellow, whose adventures have **been legion,** and escapes incredibly narrow."

"**I** am not needy, and she is artificial," said Harold, coldly.

" Nature **is** out of fashion," **said Mostyn,** almost out of patience with this impracticable savage, "and the world gets on tolerably well without her. **But since** you are so difficult, there is that little Miss Leigh Warne, the freshest thing **out, well dowered and well** favoured. Indeed, **when I** think of it, you are right. **I would give** her the preference. Widows—my dear boy —widows are the deuce! I *can't* recommend one."

" It might be the exception to prove the rule."

" No, no; risky. How is Mrs. Harnage?" inquired Mostyn, in terms of commiseration. " I have not called there lately. Do you know if it would be agreeable?"

" I see Mrs. Harnage very seldom, and cannot say whether your presence would be deemed a favour or not," replied Harold, stiffly.

" Strange—Ralph Harnage taking himself off to the Continent directly you returned," continued Mostyn, who as mouthpiece of society was bent upon gaining food for its consuming curiosity if possible. " Not a matter of regret for his wife. People *do* say—but, no, I wont distress you with idle gossip; we men of the world know how much importance is to be attached to it. But, as I always tell them, they do not know the true history of the affair. Any one could see it was one of those marriages of convenience which always turn out the most inconvenient."

"Oblige me by saying no more on a subject you cannot possibly understand," said Harold, haughtily, and dashing into his bedroom adjoining. To have his dearest, most secret feelings probed thus by society's gaudy, unthinking butterfly, was unbearable.

"Poor devil! he loves her still! another victim—another *coup manqué!*" soliloquized Mostyn, adjusting his hat to the hundredth part of an inch, and drawing on carefully his tight-fitting primrose gloves. "This is a severe case. Mine is good advice— travel is the thing; Greece is an invaluable

15—2

specific; the banditti are counter-irritants. I must toddle to my Lady Verschoyle, and tell her that I have failed to secure the newest lion for her 'At Home' to-night. This little animal positively refuses to roar at command. How his eyes gleamed when I spoke of Mrs. Harnage! I thought I should be bolted on the spot. A romance in real life! Shabby conduct of Master Ralph's—such an immaculate, nicely-spoken gentleman as he was; gave good dinners, too; and what wines! We have had the last of them."

The retrospect was too painful, and Mr. Mostyn departed not in peace with his kind.

" No good can come of it," he muttered, with a mixture of melancholy and spite. " I should advise our young friend's closing his wonderful vicissitudes by the Roman virtue—suicide. It is a graceful ending."

Society would not have approved of this extinction, that capricious dame having welcomed Harold with extended arms. All doors flew open to this interesting man, whose adventures had given him a flavour of romance (to say nothing of his literary triumphs), in addition to the subtle aroma furnished by Miser Harnage's money bags.

It is fatal to be young, rich, single, and a genius. Panderers gather around, anxious to devote themselves to his pleasures, and to the ruin of his soul. But Harold possessed safeguards that sprang directly from his misfortunes. No man could come out of such a trial the same in disposition and character. Distrust of all mankind was in his mind; his inborn lovingness remained, but it no longer leaped forth spontaneously; it was crusted with a cold reserve little likely to be penetrated by the summer friends who crowded about him. Deceit and

frivolity seemed to surround him ; he ceased
to believe in himself, for he had ceased to
believe in Eunice, his better, dearer self.
The world of imagination had become a ·
blank, his days a wearisome routine, passed
in listlessness or in false excitement that
brought no real enjoyment. It ceased to
be a satisfaction to him that he had heaped
humiliation on his enemy ; he told himself
often that he cared for nothing—not even
for her. If he could only forget ! He must
—he *would forget!*

His restlessness and inactivity in pursuit
of this praiseworthy end were surprising.
He was here, there, and everywhere.
Society, at its wit's end, did not know
where to have him, but perpetually
stumbled upon him when least expected.
He was generally at full speed—riding,
driving, or walking ; rapid locomotion appeared his craze. Society voted his eccen-
tricities charming, forgave his frequent

brusque refusals to its pet entertainments; was equally ready **to applaud** his mad gaiety of one day, **or** admire his gloomy isolation of the next. A wealthy—(the primary qualification should be stated first) —good-looking man, possessed **of** a subtle personal magnetism, and to whom **a story** attached, was a choice morsel that even sated society was inclined **to** value.

Harold tried **sincerely to do the** right thing, more for Eunice's sake than virtue's. He could not endure the thought that he who intended **to** be her guardian angel through life should prove a rock of offence —a stumbling-block **in her gentle** path; that people should **talk** about her, and take her good name in vain—rather **he** would **vow never to see** her again. **He** lacked the courage for this extreme measure; but he put a restraint upon himself, and went more and more rarely to Eaton Square. And to **a** certain **extent, this self-**

discipline was successful; he threw himself
into society, he looked after his property,
took frequent journeys to Chesney, and
altogether betrayed an aptitude for managing his own affairs which was distressing
to his lawyer and steward ; and he began
to write an account of his experiences
among savage life.

Men can defy and trample on sorrows,
they have aims and hopes outside the
home life, which round the angular lines
of their lot ; man must sweat, toil, endure,
and overcome, while it is left for women to
drain the cup of suffering to the dregs, to
wear out their hearts in forlorn longings :
there should be more women in heaven ;
their punishment mostly comes sharp and
full on earth.

A sense that she deserved her trouble
made Eunice endure it meekly, but her
grief was none the less resistless that she

bore it calmly. **The mystery of** life oppressed her, and others **better and** wiser
than Eunice have **been tempted to** think
its burthens heavy and its fates unequal.
She longed with **a** sinful weak longing to
see him, **and** was wildly anxious to make
herself **look** fair. **And her poor efforts**
made, she chafed **because he did not come.**
With **a** woman's unreason, where her affections are concerned, she did **not** recognise
that, in refraining from visiting her, he
gave the strongest proof of his **true, deep**
love. And when they did meet, they tried
in vain to find safe topics ; the one thought
uppermost in the mind of each would **start**
up at every turn in the conversation like a
ghost to scare them into silence. Scarcely
a sentence could be said that did not
somehow recal the past **and trench on**
things forbidden.

CHAPTER XX.

Had we never lov'd sae kindly,
Had we never lov'd sae blindly,
Never met, or never parted,
We had ne'er been broken hearted.

OLD SONG.

SOME days after Mostyn's visit, Harold paid one of his rare calls in Eaton Square. He started as Eunice came into the drawing-room, she had such a fragile transparent look—blue circles round her eyes strongly marked, and a curious far-off expression, as though she were gazing with the eyes of her soul after vanished happiness, striving to recover tracks of the fugitive that could never return for her in this world. They began several subjects ; but, essay what they would, it proved a conversational pitfall, and he soon rose to leave.

"Why do you wear this still?" said he, touching her sleeve. "I have seen you in nothing but black. Pardon me—I forget; it is for your brother."

"No," said Eunice, her lips quivering, "I wear it for my lost happiness."

"You look pale—have you been out to-day?" he asked, with an abrupt change of tone.

"No."

"When did you go out last?"

"I don't remember—some days ago," she answered, vaguely.

"You should drive every day; the weather is lovely. Good-bye."

She gave him her hand.

"And you will not come again for ever so long. Why are you so cold and formal?" she whispered.

" What do you mean ?"

" Do not be so hard upon me," said she, piteously.

" I do not wish to be hard—we have become strangers—you to me, and I to you."

" Yes, strangers," she repeated, despairingly ; " quite strangers, since you say so."

Like a true **lover, he** thought her yet more lovely, her head bent in grief, like a **lily** surcharged **with raindrops.** He had forced **himself to be cold, and now in a** revulsion of feeling thought that he had been *hard*—stern duties need not speak sternly.

" Come out for a walk in the Park with me, Eunice : it is not far, and you want air. **Get on** your bonnet at once, like **a** good girl."

She brightened **and** obeyed with a smile that blinded him to every other consideration, until her return in the daintiest little grey bonnet, into which Mam'selle Blanche had hastily insinuated a red rose at her mistress' suggestion (he did not seem to approve her mourning).

He offered his arm, and they walked to the Park, entering it at Albert Gate, and passing down the " Mile," where a few carriages only straggled, for it was not yet fashion's hour. They talked but little ; some unmeaning remarks on the day, the passers by; each feared to disturb memories of the past that were hidden for the moment in the enchanted haze of the present ; words were unnecessary, beyond and beside the twofold consciousness that they were alone and together.

They roamed into Kensington Gardens, down near the keeper's cottage, and duly admired his floral triumph. The beech and chestnut trees fresh in their young leaves and feathery pink blossoms, made a canopy through which gorgeous orange and purple clouds peeped their glories in the setting sun, predisposing to delicious reveries. They were not ten minutes' walk from the centre of London dissipation, and yet it would be difficult for two people to be more really alone.

It was very pleasant on the fine May-day to be walking with Eunice in this quiet spot—so pleasant, that Harold began a self-inquisition. " Why was he here ?— what would come of it ?—why had he allowed her to be entrapped into a false position ?" He saw the face so near his shoulder—the wistful eyes that met his own, and he spoke accusingly : " Why do you look at me, Eunice ?"

" Do I ? I cannot help it."

" But you must not ; it is not right," he said, harshly.

"No?" said she, inquiringly, and her eyes still lifted to his face.

"No, it tempts me," in a short sharp voice as half in pain.

Her eyes were downcast now and filled with tears, and a painful red burned over cheeks and brow.

"Is it that you are so fond of me, Eunice?" still gazing at her, as if fascinated against his will.

"Yes," said she, simply, and not raising her eyes.

"*My* Eunice—yes, *mine,*" said he in softest, tenderest tones. "Yes, look at me—for you are mine, and I am yours."

The gardens were deserted, save for a distant nursemaid and her charges, who doubtless reaped the amusement generally furnished by a pair of lovers.

Harold stopped, and framing her face in both his hands, gazed long at her with a yearning almost painful to see—a yearning that would not be quenched in the knowledge of the barrier between them. She seemed drawn and enfolded in that full glance. Then bending slowly he laid his lips on hers with a long kiss.

They walked unsteadily on. No word did they say : he looked straight before him ; the chaos that reigned in his heart and mind would not allow of orderly words. They neared the entrance of the gardens at the head of the Serpentine, and smart carriages rolled frequently by ; the sight recalled to Harold the world and the world's opinion which he so greatly dreaded for her. He had been weak, wrong, and he would never again be drawn into temptation ; he would watch over her welfare, but it must be from a distance.

" Eunice, forgive me," said he, in the slow serious voice of decision. " I ask your forgiveness, for **I** have behaved unpardonably **to you.** **It has only taught** me what I knew before—my own weakness **in** all that concerns you. We must not meet any more."

"*Never?*" **said** Eunice, incredulous of her ears.

"Never is a long day," said he, sadly, "but **I** think **we** had better consider it *never* at present. **It is** best we **should not** see each other—I mistrust myself."

Eunice's heart died within **her**; she **felt** as if **she, a** warm sentient creature, **were** entering her tomb; but she had no thought of combating his resolve ; **virtues, and** the ideas and words **that** signify **them, subdue** more invincibly **than battle-axes.**

"**You** are right, Harold," said she, **firmly, her young** face full of tragic earnestness.

A barouche with yellow wheels and brown

liveries, with high-stepping black horses, came dashing along.

"There is the Verschoyles' carriage!" said Harold, hastily. "Good-bye—I will leave you ; you can easily find your way home from here.—Go that way."

She turned off at his bidding, and walked hurriedly in the direction he pointed out, putting down her veil to hide the scalding tears of humiliation and dismay : to her inexperience his conduct was strained and unreasonable. She struck off across a quiet footpath away from the drive, and glancing back, saw the Verschoyles' carriage was stationary, and that Harold leaned into it talking to two ladies.

CHAPTER XXI.

Say, what remains when hope is fled ?
She answered, " Endless weeping !"

IF he could only forget !—a beaker of the waters of Lethe must be swallowed — at any cost he would master the lesson of oblivion that is wont to come so easily to the world's tenants—the lesson that every law of the universe demonstrates untiringly ; light succeeds to darkness ; winter to summer ; the storm exhausts its vehemence, and serenity again reigns. And Harold resolved that joy should yet replace and blot out his sorrow. Ralph's suggestion was like an evil spirit that sought to nestle in his soul ; but he would not be lured into wrong; never by his means should the angel who loved him become one of Passion's lost daughters.

If he could only forget! Clearly his best hope was to find a new object—if he married it would be a safeguard for them both; it would silence gossip, and enable him to be a true valuable friend to her. These strong incentives before him, Harold went everywhere—except to Eaton Square, and only the shade of stern sorrow that settled on his face told what that exception cost him; and he honestly did his best to second the exertions of more than one aspiring belle. But he found that his taste had grown critical; even where his eye acknowledged beauty, no fire was kindled in his heart. Unhappily his nature was constant, and habit of thought had made Eunice a part of his life—of his religion. After a time he gave up the project of providing her a rival, but not before his name had been coupled with Miss Leigh Warne's, and a paragraph had found its way into the *Post.*

Eunice meanwhile did not fare well. Some natures do best in prosperity ; others never show so brightly as in gloomy days. Eunice was a fair-weather flower ; like a sensitive plant she shrunk up, withered under the chilling blast that might have invigorated a more robust character. A continual fever of shame and self-reproach wasted her ; " what hath been and never more can be" was present with her always, poisoning her life with regrets. She regarded everything connected with her marriage, remotely or otherwise, with a helpless shuddering disgust ;—and it was her own handiwork ! In this was her greatest suffering, that her own act had riveted her life's misery. And the shame

was on her that he would not come to see
her because he mistrusted her, he thought
her foolishly, wickedly fond.   If anything
could have cured her, it would have been
this humiliating conviction ; but it only
helped to weigh her to the earth—to make
her realize that her whole being had been
crushed out in this one love.

As time went on, she felt shame, too, of
her equivocal position before the servants,
who were, however, the quintessence of
respect.   (Harold had managed to intimate
that it was desirable to show her all consideration.)   She went through the routine
of existence : eat, drank, and put her
raiment on. Certainly she did not sleep
much—the nights were worse than the
days.   Luncheon was the great trial ; she
had no appetite for the fine meal that was
daily provided and scrupulously served ;
the large room struck a chill as she entered

it, feeling a prisoner to the servants—the butler and footman who were in **attendance,** and who observed her until she **felt a** mouthful would choke her.   Breakfast and tea were comparatively peaceful, for she partook of them in solitude—late dinner she had early discarded as an unnecessary ceremony.

The whole staff of servants were kept as usual, the only one dismissed being **Mr.** Harnage's own man.   The **respectable** housekeeper continued to discharge her functions, and Eunice was troubled by **no** bills.   Of course she knew who was looking after her, and in a way it pleased her to be dependent upon him, though had he given her bread and water, she would have been equally satisfied **as** long **as it** came from him.

Personal news of any dear friend—one in whom we are specially interested, is

pretty sure to filter its way quickly to our
eager ears, and Eunice in the solitude of
her big house was not long ignorant of the
rumour that Harold was engaged to Miss
Leigh Warne. He had not called since
their one walk !—this then was the reason.
He would not even tell her, but left her to
hear what concerned him so nearly from
the indifferent.

"Oh ! what shall I do ?—where shall I
go ?—how end my wretched days ?" she
asked herself, despairingly. Her love-
dreams were closed, her life's brief story
ended ; all memories belonging to her were
swept utterly away into the chambers of
the past. An unselfish woman would wish
it ; she ought to rejoice. "The past is
dead and gone for ever," she repeated
wearily again and again. "Oh ! would
that I, too, might die !"

She wanted to be at rest—away from

this never-ending misery ; she was of no use in the world, only a drag upon Harold. To hope for a diviner life beyond the grave is the boon granted to poor humanity, and the very darkness that hides from us the charms of earth beneficently displays to our upward gaze the glory of the heavens.

Eunice gave orders she was at home to no one ; she might have spared the trouble —few called. It is difficult to imagine any young creature more friendless, who, yet in the world, was more cruelly shut off from its sympathies. If the earth had opened and swallowed him up, Ralph Harnage could not have disappeared more completely from her life ; weeks, months went by, but he gave no sign of his existence. A country girl, just introduced to some of Mr. Harnage's set, Eunice's acquaintances were few—friends she had none ! And she had not written of her troubles to Grantley ; it could do no good ; the idea of her stepmother's false commiseration was abhorrent, and her father in his hopelessly imbecile state could no longer give or take comfort.

Midsummer had deepened into the hottest edition of the dog-days ever known in England, and Eunice faded gradually. London was emptying fast beneath the thinning influence of a scorching July, and Harold thought he would go away, try the air of the Engadine, which he understood was so bracing that it would be impossible to feel low-spirited. He must say good-bye to Eunice ; it was his duty to see that she was well before he left England ; he would ascertain her plans, whether she intended to visit her father : and, above all, there lurked in the background of his mind, that he would offer her husband's return. He could not bring himself to face the idea boldly; he tried vainly to remember that it is divine to forgive injuries, that we should love the man even in the murderer; vengeance still burned within him an unslaked **thirst**; nor could he think it would be for her happiness to reunite her to such **a man.**

He went at noon, wishing to **make** sure of finding **her at home.** He little knew that she never went out, that the carriage and horses still at her disposal had a sine-cure appointment; **the** coachman, **who had** come to regard the calling **for** orders as a mere empty form from which nothing re-sulted, having studiously **kept** his ex-periences in his own breast.

As Harold rang the bell, he thought of **the** sweet smile she always wore for him. **He** scarcely knew whether he **most hated** or longed to see her, which he could never

do without a gnawing regret for the good
for ever lost.   He was unexpected, and
found her with evident traces of tears.   He
had not seen her for several weeks, and the
change in her appearance struck him for-
cibly as she rose to greet him, her principal
care to hide that she had been crying.

" Eunice !—you are ill !—I am sure of
it," he exclaimed, retaining her hand in his
anxiety.

" No, no ; it is nothing.   I am—quite
well," she stammered.   " I have not seen
you for so long, you have forgotten what I
am like."   The change had come so
gradually, that she had no notion how
much she was altered.

" But you know why I have stayed
away, Eunice ?" said he, in his gentlest
voice, an indescribable pity softening his
dark face.

" Oh ! yes, I know ; or I can guess,

which is nearly the same thing. **You have** come to tell me the news. I am **to** congratulate you."

" Really—on what ?"

" Your engagement to Miss Warne."

" You must make a better guess, Eunice ; that **one is** wide of the mark. **I** heard yesterday Miss Warne **is** to be the new Countess of Clevedon. Money is a sun casting shadows in which men's reputations are greatly magnified ; but you rate **my** performances too high—I cannot compete with my Lord Clevedon."

" **And** you are not sorry—not—disappointed ?" she hesitated, scarcely knowing what to make of his manner.

" **Not a jot;** she has not even left me **the luxury of** a grievance. I never had any pretensions ; it is the merest babble of gossip-mongers. **But let us** talk of yourself. **Why** do you **look so ill** ?"

"Do I? it must be the hot weather; London is rather trying."

"Yes; town is unbearable. I am going away, and I want you to go to Grantley—go home for a time."

"No," said she, hastily, "I cannot go there—I will never go there again."

"Then what do you say to Eastbourne or Hastings?" said he, finding excuse for her apparent want of natural affection in the thought that Grantley would be painful from its past happy memories. "Do go, to please me. Your friend, Mrs. Grey, I daresay, could accompany you."

"Yes, perhaps she might," assented Eunice, indifferently; "but I would rather stay here. I like it best."

"A wilful woman, Eunice. But you must at least take more care of yourself. Would you—like—me to send—for him—for Ralph?" he continued, after a pause.

His anxiety increased as he studied her looks. "I will do even that to please you."

"Not for the world ! it would kill me to see him again !" she exclaimed vehemently, and turning deadly pale. "I am so silly. You gave me a fright ; but, please, never mention it again."

"Very well," said he, soothingly. "But if you will look so ill you must have a doctor."

"I am not ill. Don't think of me. I am a trouble to you, to every one. I wish I could help it—that I could help myself," her dejected tones speaking her inward wretchedness.

"You are never a trouble to me, Eunice. If I could only see you bright and joyous again, I would consent to eternal estrangement."

"Where do you mean to go ?" she asked,

as he sat looking at her without attempting further conversation.

"To—to Chesney," said he, suddenly substituting his country-house for the more ambitious tour abroad. "I have matters there that require attention. I have been busy getting my new book ready, or I should have seen you before."

"Will it be out soon?"

"Almost immediately."

"It is sure to be a success; your name is made," said she, confidently.

"I daresay. As Sterne says of the decayed nobleman, true merit in my case must be allowed to have 'fought up against its condition with great firmness.' I like to write," he continued, dreamily; "it is good to have something to do—it prevents thinking."

"Yes; that is where men are so much more fortunate than women. *I* have nothing to do. If I had my living to earn it would be better for me."

" You do not look very fit for hard work. What would be best for you just now is a little country air. I cannot go away unless you will promise me to go to the sea."

" Perhaps you are right ; and indeed I will go," said Eunice, seeing his earnestness.

" Can I do anything in engaging rooms ?"

"Oh no ; Mrs. Grey will arrange that."

" And you will send for me if you want anything ?" said he, still disturbed about her health.

" Yes," said she, mechanically.

And then he went.

A whirl of physical exertion was his only chance to drive away the pale, careworn face that haunted him. He threw himself into a hansom and drove straight to the railway, resting not till he found himself at Chesney.

CHAPTER XXII.

Though the mills of **God** grind slowly, yet they grind
    exceeding small;
Though with patience **He** stands waiting, with exactness grinds He all.—LONGFELLOW.

THE heat became more intense : such a hot summer had not been known to visit our northern clime within the memory of man. There seemed to be no principle of life in the suffocating air which swept heavily over the dusty roads and pavement like a blast from a furnace ; not a drop of rain had gladdened weary Londoners for several weeks. One saw dust, breathed dust, looked dust, until one felt persuaded that London might compete with Sahara for dusty horrors ; it was so importunate in its discomforts that it became engrossing, and the mind could only

dwell on **this** infinitesimal misery which
was so great.

Eunice from the window regarded with
mournful eyes the closed shutters—some
encased in careful newspapers—of her absent neighbours. **The** drawing-room was
close and hot as **an** oven with the fire just
withdrawn, and she went out, fancying she
should gasp more freely in the Square
garden. But it was a choice between staying indoors to be suffocated, or going out to
be actively broiled. **All** was insufferably
bright—no shade ; shrubs and grass and
flowers, alike dried up and arid, had assumed
a sable in place of green hue, every bit of
sweetness they once possessed choked up
in a **smell of** concentrated blacks.

Eunice left the square, walked down
Arabella Row, through St. James's Park,
into Pall **Mall.** **The** streets were a blank
except for the cabmen, who " weak but in-

17—2

trepid, sad but unsubdued," still dared the imminent sunstroke in the hope of getting a fare. Carriages no longer rolled their fashionable occupants on their various errands ; the business man and thrifty tradesman had alike loosed their chains from this huge Babylon ; the busy mocking spirits that give it life had fled to verdant pastures—to the cool big sea, forgetting their crafty handiwork in an innocent dallying with shells and sparkling waves.

It made Eunice thirsty to think of the sea as she dragged her heavy languid steps —she pictured sweet, refreshing sylvan scenes, until she longed for a sight of the country, for glistening cool waters and the shade of deep woods.

At last she reached her destination. The hospital was very quiet ; it was not an ordinary visitors' day, and only a medical man or some habitué of the place, intent on good works, moved silently in and out of the large portal. Eunice had often visited the women's side, but always shirked the men's wards ; she could not bear to see the gaunt unshaven faces of the stricken bread-winners, and she followed a Sister hurriedly past the long line of beds.

" You received my letter, Mrs. Harnage ?"

" Yes."

" I am glad you have come," said Sister Prudentia. " Young Robinson is so anxious to see and to thank you for your kindness, that I believe it would affect his convalescence if he were disappointed."

" And will he be able to work again ?"

" He is going to our place in the country to-morrow for a fortnight, and the doctors promise that he will return a perfectly sound man."

" How glad his wife and children will be ! I knew them well at Grantley."

A dull hollow sound—could it be an echo of her old name that she heard? It must be fancy. Her head was downcast, and a veil, spite of the heat, hid the sweet face—how unlikely that she should be recognised.

"Eunice! Miss Grantley!" moaned a voice from a bed near.

She turned, and gazed for a moment incredulous of her eyes. Was that wreck of a man, with the dews of pain on his brow, and skin hanging loosely on the fleshless cheeks, with dull eyes and flaccid muscles, and large gaunt hands clutching at the bedclothes—Morell Pyke?

She went up to him.

"You know me?" he asked.

She looked sadly at him, as her lips formed an affirmative.

"I am dying!" he said, in a broken voice; "dying a dog's death in this dog's hole—dying of that **terrible** disease, that spreading, gnawing, devouring agony, cancer. Come nearer! You are the first old friend **I** have seen here. You **wonder** to find me thus. **But** I was determined **to** come home. **What a** coming home!—**and** what a death, after what a life!—**to die by bits of inches!**" He panted out the words in short sentences, as **his** wasted **limbs moved** restlessly.

"Cannot I do **something for you?**" said Eunice, gently. "Have **you** no friends?"

"*Not one!*" said he, almost fiercely. "Not **one of** those **insects who fluttered in** the sunshine of my wealth would **come** near me now. Serves me right—serves me right!" he repeated, wearily. "**I** have lived for the world, and I have got my wages. I got **into** trouble **over** there—the worst mess I was ever in—and I was fixed to leave that infernal country. I hadn't a stiver, and I worked my way over." He plucked continually at the bedclothes, as if he found it impossible to keep quiet. " It has done my business—finished me. But serve me right!—the end—will—come— soon"—and he lay back exhausted on the pillow.

" Do not talk ; it excites you ; you may get better."

"Never—never—I do not—wish it. Life—is—" He lapsed into a semi-uncon- sciousness, paralysed by pain.

Eunice was shocked at his palpable agonies.

" A hopeless case," whispered the Sister ; " it can be only a matter of days."

Eunice visited Pyke again and again ; it pleased him to see her, and she could not refuse to soothe one who suffered so terribly. His complaint made rapid strides, and death seemed ever at hand, and yet delayed to make the final step. It would seem as if God in His wisdom gives men some foretastes of punishment in these dreadful diseases, that they may be alive to its terrors and repent while there is yet time.

Eunice told herself that she was glad Harold had gone away; but as the days passed and not even a line came from him, she fretted and cried more unrestrainedly than ever, and she began to feel ill. Her solitary life, interrupted only by visits to the hospital, tended to depress her vital energies. There is no tyrant like habit, or one who more seldom relaxes his power once established; and Eunice had thoroughly contracted the habit of being unhappy. The jealousy that had torn her during the last two months had been set at rest by

Harold's assurance that she had no rival ; yet her spirits did not recover their elasticity. She moved about in a nightmare ; she no longer seemed to be herself; the Eunice she knew was gone, and in her place had come a shadow, a wretched blighted thing, whose case was beyond all remedy.

She had meant to keep her promise and go into the country, but Pyke implored the charity of her presence ; and Mrs. Grey had been called to attend a sick relative, and Eunice lacked the courage to leave home alone ; so she stayed on and on in London, and soon she was too ill to dream of taking journeys. A great restlessness came upon her, and she wandered incessantly over the large house, upstairs and down, as if seeking rest, but finding none in the hot glaring rooms where the perpetual sunshine mocked her attempts to find darkness. And in the short nights, she tossed vainly from side to side, calling on sleep to return and give her blessed forgetfulness.

CHAPTER XXIII.

Alone!—that worn-out word,
So idly spoken, and so coldly heard;
Yet all that poets sing, and grief hath known,
Of hopes laid waste, knells in that word—Alone!

BULWER LYTTON.

IN the most favoured corner of the lake country, amid loveliness that baffles description, upon smooth-shaven ground, buried in trees and facing the blue lake, stood the superb house Ralph Harnage had purchased in the pride of his wealth.

Harold summoned companions around him, hoping in their gay converse to banish the pale face that haunted him. Then with thinly veiled excuses, he as abruptly dismissed them from the joys and relaxa-

tions of Chesney ; **he wanted** to be quiet,
to **think** of *her*—when did he not think of
her ?

And now he had his wish. In the **closing** of the summer's day he walked alone
under the shadow of the stately trees—
magnificent **timber,** oaks that might build
a navy. **And** he looked up at the handsome mansion and **down on the green vales
and** sweeping woods, **but they** brought no
pleasure, for his hearth was cold and empty,
and his heart was filled with the **image** of
one whom it was sin to love. **And Harold**
groaned, **" Why did I** ever leave her ?"
This inheritance, for which her people sold
her into a bondage **worse** than death—how
he hated it ! A tithe, a twentieth part
given with **an** open hand before he went
to India, would have saved them both ; they
would never have been **separated.** The
miser's gold, intended to insure their hap-

piness, had brought a curse instead of a blessing—had proved a direct agent in their undoing.

Loaded with riches, his capacity to enjoy them was gone. His last book had had an immediate and extraordinary success; the fame he would five years ago have given worlds to secure, was in his grasp; but the eagerly desired flower, though in its first bloom, was for him already withered and worthless as a dead leaf. This mockery of aspirations realized only filled him with a keener sense of desolation; his destiny was accomplished and yet unfulfilled. How far it had fallen short of his early imaginings!

Silence and loneliness have a power of summoning the trackless phantoms of buried **thoughts.** He did not know how it was, but this evening there came a resurrection of things and times for ever past and gone. **He** saw Eunice half-child, half-woman, sportive and merry and loving—ah! how loving to him, who had brought her nothing but trouble and misery. A phantasmagoria of his past life was conjured up in the gloaming made visible by the magic of a memory that would not die : some flashed upon him like fierce spirits, and seemed to glare and threaten; others, more gentle, smiled pitifully; and now a familiar form floated before him, a figure in white with sad beseeching eyes and tangled hair, and with outstretched hands approached him in the haze of twilight. He started to meet it, and the vision dissolved into nothing.

Was she ill ? He remembered her forlorn condition. Surely she had kept her promise and gone to the sea. He felt remorseful, uneasy about her ; the smouldering resentment which he had tried to **keep alive that it** might prove an incentive to right conduct, was entirely subdued to pity,

and a glow of repentant tenderness flushed
his dark cheek. He had been hard on her
—on his poor Eunice. She was his yet—
his very own in spirit. How his love had
clouded her young life! begun in deceit,
nourished in secrecy, its sweetness had
turned to ashes between his teeth ; it had
withered before ever it came to maturity.
He found her a child, beautiful, full of
joyousness, and what was her life now ?
His heart bled to think how desolate she
was—and he had left her !

He began to question whether the **Power**
which guides man through the ages was,
after all, guiding him aright. He was sure
that she was very unhappy ; she looked so
that last day : perhaps even now she
thought he had ceased to care for her. **He**
stood, self-accused of the veriest hard-
heartedness. He would go up and see her
the very next day, and he would comfort

her, and let her see the truth that she was all in all to him **as** in the old days. He was sick of this pretence of friendship. **He** had sworn to love and cherish her years **ago,** and he would keep his oath against any fatality : she was *his ;* he had thought of her as his **wife for** five long years. **It** came upon **him** like **a** devouring thirst that he must speak, must **hold her in** his arms, and feel her soft cheek **against his own : and** he feared **no** repulse ; he knew **he** reigned **supreme in** that **one breast. He did not** think of consequences beyond—he **dared** not.

A liveried servant came out of the house, **and** threaded **the** walks **bordered by** flowering shrubs, clumps of roses and fuchsia-trees, festooned with woodbine, and standing leisurely on the **chain bridge,** glanced inquiringly around, while the swans held their graceful course on the **gently** flowing water : then catching sight of the object of his search, he walked forward, and his master saw that he held a large orange-coloured envelope.

Nothing alarming about a telegram in these days, yet Harold felt at once that it was from Eunice, and with bad news, or she would not have sent to him.

His fears were true prophets. Dismissing the servant, he opened it and gazed on the message.

From Dr. Hall, **Eaton Square, London,** *to Harold Harnage, Esq., Chesney, Westmoreland.*

Mrs Harnage very ill   Bad form of low fever   In great danger   Come at once   She asks for you.

There it was, short and concise : pains had been taken to state all necessary facts, and yet not exceed the twenty words a shilling would carry. Admirable economy —why should the intelligence be softened for his benefit?—he was not her husband, and whether an aunt by marriage died or not must be a very secondary matter.

He tore into the house ; ordered his horse ; and in ten minutes was on his way to the station. Never had that eight miles been traversed so quickly : the passers-by started aside at the sound of the clattering hoofs, wondering at the mad haste which directed that reckless pace. He just caught the up night mail !

18—2

CHAPTER XXIV.

Chi ama, qual chi muore,
Non ha da gire al ciel dal mondo altr' ale.
MICHAEL ANGELO.

Death and love are the two wings which bear man
from earth to heaven.

A ROSE, pearl-like tint crept over the east, chasing the grey shadows that still lingered in the western sky when Harold entered London. That brief summer's night had been long with agony; he tried repeatedly to shorten the minutes by prayer, but a fearful tightness across his chest prevented consecutive thought.

Dazed and worn, with a sinking heart,

and a face heavy with the worst anticipations, he reached Eaton Square.

" Is she alive ?" were his first words.

" Yes."

The monosyllable brought inexpressible
relief : if life remained, his love should
avail to keep it, her spirit would listen to
his entreaties and stay to bless him.

In the ante-room he met the doctor.

" How is she ? Is she very ill ?"—his
dry lips scarcely able to frame the inquiry.

" Mrs. Harnage is very ill ; she has been
sinking steadily every hour ; but she lives,
and the delirium has passed.

" But there is hope ?"

" I am sorry to say—*none;* she cannot
possibly rally. She has evidently been
unhappy, and, in my opinion, distress of
mind has lowered the system and sapped
its recuperative powers. Her desire to see
you has alone kept her alive till now."

The professional man regarded Harold curiously, as he passed on, heartbroken, into the stately chamber where Eunice lay, pale and wasted—her large, sunken eyes following the servant's movements as she walked softly about the room. The sheets were scarcely whiter than her face, and her disordered hair hung in dark heavy rings, making the wan cheeks look like chiselled marble.

He went forward and fell on his knees, with a gesture of unutterable anguish, kissing the hand she languidly extended. The nurse left the room, closing the door.

When we are solitary, we are on the road to become companions of God; and these weeks of solitude and suffering had purified Eunice—face to face with that deliverer, Death, she felt no fears. She wore a serene and peaceful look: the painful breathing softened at the sight of him, and a glow of

happiness transfigured her face ; her eyes lighted up, and her lips parted—breathless to speak last words of love.

" Harold, good boy **to come**" (she loved to praise him). " I knew that you would come, though you have not loved me lately —not—as you used to. But you will for- give me, now that **I am going away**," said she, sweetly pleading.

" Oh, **my Eunice, don't talk like that, it** kills me ! Live—live **for my** sake ! **I love you more** than **ever—I cannot live** without you !" And **he bent** over her, agonized—his pallid complexion lending a darker shade **to** his eyes, wild with misery.

She turned slowly, and with difficulty. " Closer," she whispered.

Death is drawing nearer ; he is touching that pale face ; he **is** busy pinioning those **gentle hands ; but** she weakly **tries to** oppose **his power, and, love** triumphing, she raises them with a mighty effort, and puts her arms round Harold's neck.

"Take me in your arms, Harold. I cannot raise myself." He obeyed : a smile played round her mouth, and as he kissed her again and again, she said in low tones —"I have my wish, what I have prayed for night and day since you came back, that I might die in your arms."

"Do not cry, dearest," said she, presently, "when I am glad of everything. It is all over now."

The pain, the sorrow, and the shame were past ; only joy remained, the dearer that it had come after much suffering.

"You will leave me, Eunice? I must part with you?" his words were the embodiment of sad hopelessness.

"To live is to struggle and suffer, while to die is rest and peace," she murmured.

He spoke not—moved not, but knelt

there a statue in **his** despair, his hands cold, his lips pale as the **loved** one whose last life's hue he watched fading away.

When she spoke again it was in an exhausted voice.

"Bury my ring with me—your ring; it is large for me now. ' I have to be careful to keep it on. **You** would cease to love me if I lost it; and I do not want you to forget me. **Do you know**, Harold," said she, mysteriously, "**I** burned the other ring! **I** am sorry—it was wicked. I only have been to blame; forgive him—Ralph. Say that you will."

He forced a smile—such a smile! "I would do anything you asked of me. **I** see that I have been revengeful, **ill-advised.** It would have been better for you had he stayed here." His voice so poignant in self-reproach, seemed to pierce the haze that gathered round about **her.**

" No, my dearest, it is all for the best,"
said she, faintly. "Don't grieve, dearest,
when I am so happy."

" Happy to leave me, Eunice ?" said he,
almost choked by his sobs.

" Mine could be only a living death. I
must die to live ; your life will be
brighter and happier without me." She
was silent, and closed her eyes, panting
feebly.

He watched her, he knew not for how
long, never taking his eyes from the dear
face that lay on his shoulder, every line im-
printed and burnt into his memory in those
sad minutes.

" I shiver—it grows dark. I cannot see
you well." Her voice had grown fainter,
and sounded as if from a distance. "But
beautiful images shine yonder, brighter yet.
There—meet me there, Harold," opening
her eyes wide on him. Her respiration

became feebler, and **with a great effort** she said, **"God** for ever bless you ! Heaven **take my** soul."

He felt her become heavier in his arms : her breath came **more slowly** and laboriously for some minutes, and then all **was over.**

He was alone!

The wanderer had **reached the haven of** happiness—the restless **had found rest.**

Not as man sees, seeth God ;
Not as man loves, loveth He ;
When the dregs-stained lips are failing,
When **the** tear-spent eyes are veiling,
Dawns eternity.

THE END.

LONDON:

SAVILL, EDWARDS AND CO., PRINTERS, CHANDOS STREET,
COVENT GARDEN.

www.ingramcontent.com/pod-product-compliance
Lightning Source LLC
Chambersburg PA
CBHW020900020726
47497CB00005B/1501